THE CHIEF KILLER

DANIEL BYRAM

SIERRA WEST BOOKS

PRINT
ISBN-13: 9781892798497

Cover design by: Art Painter
Library of Congress Control Number: 2018675309
Printed in the United States of America

editorial: R. Lewis

CONTENTS

FORWARD

First, this story is a complete and total work of fiction. The City of Mesa is a real place, and yes, I did work there many years ago. I retired from there having spent most of my years working in the intelligence and special investigations units. That's where the reality ends.

But the story does touch on some issues modern law enforcement in general faces every day. In today's world, every police agency and city government seems to be plagued with a few universal problems. In this story, I attempt... never mind, I'll let you decide if I attempt to do anything beyond dark humor, mystery, and action sets.

In spite of what the story suggests, as of this writing, Mesa PD has a Chief promoted from within and has the lowest crime rate of any city of its size in the country. I don't think those two facts are a coincidence.

I'm proud of the Mesa Police Department and honored to have been part of it. They have gone through tough patches occasionally, like every police agency, yet they continue to work through every obstacle and come out stronger on the other side. In the course of carrying out their duties, from time to time, although rarely, someone or something fails and the results can be horrible. It happens in a business which deals in life and death situations routinely. And when it happens, that negative story is what gets amplified and recorded for posterity, not the millions of hours of good police work done. When our officers are constantly under a microscope, scrutinized, and mischaracterized by the press, opportunistic political operatives, and self-serving activists, it's tough for everyone to see them as the good guys. But these fine officers still suit up and go out there every shift to protect us, and I am deeply grateful for each and every one of them.

Thank you, officers and civilians of Mesa PD,

Dan

Author's note: all characters, events, names, places, businesses, people, institutions, and agencies in this story are fictitious or are used fictitiously. The companies owning any products named or described herein do not endorse this story and I do not endorse, market, or recommend any product. If I happened to mention some product or place in the book, it's probably because I think it's very cool and it helps advance the character or location development. As mentioned, this is an absolute and total work of fiction created for entertainment purposes only, designed for a very specific and elite group of bright and articulate people who require a special kind of off-the-wall dark humor. If you are offended or upset by anything the characters in this story, say or do, please remember these literally come from the equivalent of voices in my head. Relax and enjoy. It's simply a tall tale. Have fun and enjoy the reality break.

DEDICATION

Joseph Wambaugh

January 22, 1937 - February 28, 2025

Rest in peace, Sergeant

PROLOGUE

K-9 Officer Bill Kent was having a slow night, so he and his dog worked alleys around the downtown business district, sniffing for trouble. Finding a broken lock or window and doing a building search might score the adrenaline boost they needed to stay awake until the end of shift at five this morning.

The dog alerted. Bill instantly knew what they found.

"Shit."

Bill's fantasy of being in bed in a few hours just collapsed like a dynamited building.

He transmitted on his radio, shouting over the barking dog. "Dispatch, I need a secure channel."

"Channel five."

The officer and dispatcher switched to five.

"Send a supervisor, the watch commander, and notify homicide. A nude body. Forehead smash. Drenched in bleach. Behind a dumpster."

Bill Kent didn't recall how many bodies like this there had been downtown. For some reason there was a total lockdown on any information about them. No press, no briefings. But through the cop rumor mill, he knew there had been a lot. And now, he'd be on this fiasco until at least noon. The first officer on the scene always gets screwed on these things. You don't do any meaningful work, but the brass keeps the first officer at the scene on site until the very end in case they think of something to ask, which they never do.

Technically my report could say 'found dead body, secured same' with a time and date. That would cover every detail I know or ever will know.

He gave the location, then walked back to his car to safely secure his dog and get a roll of crime scene tape.

Lake Havasu City, Arizona

Retired Mesa Police Lieutenant Frank Bailey, stood on the bow of his old twenty-six-foot sailboat, alone on the calm waters of Lake Havasu. The anchor was set, and the sails furled.

Bailey spoke to the lake, over the spot where just a month before, he spread the ashes of his wife. "I remember the day we retired and made this place our home. It's like it was yesterday. Where did thirty years go?"

He stuffed his hands in his pockets as he gazed over the setting sun's yellow and green light show dancing on the lake and smiled. His tears were used up. There was one last thing to say, one final piece of news he needed to share before his life changed. "I'm going back to Mesa, at least for now. I don't think I can be here without you. I'm not sure I can be anywhere without you. I just think I need to get away for a while." He took a deep breath like he was a crook ready to confess a crime, then continued. "Don't worry about me, I'll be with you soon enough. But I need to go. It wouldn't hurt me to see my old police department buddies again, whoever is left, while they're still alive. And I promise, this time, I'm not going to go to the PD and be a big pain in the ass or stir up any shit." He smiled. "I'll be on my best behavior."

A sudden breeze blew over the lake, rocking the boat, forcing Frank to grab the forestay to catch his balance. Frank swore he heard the word *bullshit* and his wife's laughter.

CHAPTER 1

Mesa, Arizona - The Return

Glass, stainless steel, gray industrial linoleum floors, neon-colored fixtures, a line of cranky people, and a stressed-out employee... all the required ingredients of a franchise establishment were in place. Nothing about this facility appeared conducive to mental health. But storage locker businesses were not known for peace and tranquility, so none of this was a surprise to Frank Bailey.

The manager, a middle-aged man in an orange vest, held post at a chest-high counter while demonstrating all the enthusiasm of an inmate standing on the gallows awaiting his neck size measurement.

It was obvious this man was the manager. The word *manager* was written in black with large block letters on his vest. He had no name plate because manager positions were a high turnover job, and name tags were a poor investment. He didn't get a name tag, just manager, or boss, except there was no one else there to boss... he managed himself. At least until he either quit or chose to climb up onto the roof and leap off the edge to his death.

There *was* a fat lady who came in on weekends to assist during the busy hours. She brought halitosis and body odor along with an unwelcome willingness to discuss what happened on The View during the week.

Managing a downtown Mesa, Arizona storage locker

facility was not what one would call a *dream job* at a *destination* location. At least it had air conditioning, and the janitorial service kept the bathroom acceptably clean. The manager knew his glory days as a big box consumer electronics store director of operations was as shuttered as all seven of the former greater Phoenix locations of the once ubiquitous retail giant. Now, he's no longer a rising junior corporate executive, but just *Manager*, no name, not even a number.

His fate was sealed... no name, dead end job, obnoxious customers, trapped in Mesa, Arizona until death.

Dehumanization: complete.

"What do you need, sir?" the manager asked flatly, addressing the first person in the line of waiting customers, while scribbling on a company pad without looking up, avoiding eye contact.

An odd blubbery male in mismatched clothing sporting a mail-order haircut answered with the expected, "A storage locker?" phrasing it with such a degree of uncertainty a listener might assume the man was guessing why he was there.

The Frank Bailey patiently waiting behind the customer in line thought to himself, w*hat else would this butt hole need in a storage unit business?*

Still scribbling, the manager dutifully asked, "What size?" without expressing interest, enthusiasm, or even a will to live.

Squirming awkwardly as he adjusted his private parts, the malodorous customer vigorously scratched his groin as he stared back for an awkwardly long moment. Then, he countered with a question of his own. "What sizes do you have?"

Bailey rolled his eyes. *Is it just me, or does patience just diminish with age?* He closed his eyes and thought, *I need a drink.*

The manager didn't look up. It was routine. If he learned anything during his two long years in the storage game, it was no one seems to know why they walk into a storage unit business, or what items they want to store, or how much space they need, until you pull the information out of them like a Guantanamo interrogator. "What do you need to store, sir?"

"About seventy-five cats."

In line behind Cat Dude, Bailey wondered, *why is the same guy in my line... every line... every time... every everyplace I go?* He scanned the area for a 'no smoking' sign and fumbled around with the pack of Lucky Strikes in his jacket pocket. *maybe a cigarette might drown the stench of cat urine and lunatic perspiration coming off of this turd.* He took out a cigarette and twirled it in his fingers, glancing around surreptitiously, waiting to be scolded by any random HOA president or vegans present.

No one reacted. He waited, concealing the cigarette in his hand. Bailey eyeballed Cat Dude. *Not judging, but a fat slob in flip flops, sweatpants, a purple button-down oxford dress shirt, a sleeveless army jacket, and a black cowboy hat doesn't exactly shout out Springtime in Milan... or does it?*

The storage facility manager remained cool and detached as he replied to the cat man. "You need a boarding facility, sir. Not a storage locker. We don't take anything that's alive here."

The customer shook his head. "Oh, they aren't alive."

Bailey waiting behind Cat Dude no longer cared if smoking was permitted. He popped the heater in the corner of his mouth and torched it. *Yeah,* he pondered, *I'm definitely back in Mesa.*

The manager stared blankly at the customer. He blinked once, then replied, "Sir, you can't store *dead* cats here either."

The customer stiffened and became alarming agitated. "That's racist," the disheveled customer spat out a bit louder than necessary. A dribble of foamy drool trickled along the side of his mouth.

Manager couldn't fully process the accusation. "What?"

Cat Dude hissed, "You heard me, Hitler!"

The customer's bugged-out eyes and profuse sweating suggested some form of hallucinogenic drug was kicking in like a tidal wave in a shallow harbor. The manager suddenly realized he was in a conversation with a highly doped-up and deranged street bum. Or as the enlightened class might prefer to call him, a dis-enhoused chronic urban outdoorsman with substance abuse issues currently experiencing an out-of-body episode. Or is it outdoors-person?

The manager stood his ground as resolutely as a Floridian with a M1 Garand. "I don't know if that is racist or not, but it's company policy, sir, and I'm afraid I'm going to have to ask you to leave the store."

The manager assumed a stance worthy of a civil war statue and heroically pointed at the door, jaw set, shoulders back, and round manager belly somewhat sucked in, asserting absolute authority over his Broadway General Storage and Rental Unit Center Incorporated location, as was his destiny. For the first time in a long time, he felt like District Manager material again!

In a fit of inexplicable rage, the fat, slobbering, compiler of dead cats lifted his face to the ceiling, emitted an extended cinematic-style battle scream. He ripped his shirt open sending buttons everywhere and attempted to launch himself over the counter in a single bound like a superhero.

The manager threw his hands up and shrieked in terror like a teenage girl finding a mouse in her undies drawer.

Cat Dude felt mighty as well. In his drug addled mind, he was an avenging bat monster about to fly across the galaxy and eat an entire solar system. But rather than clearing the counter and ripping the manager's eyeballs out and eating them as he imagined, the hallucinating bum tripped over his own feet and fell forward, cracking his chin solidly on the edge of the stainless-steel counter. He wasn't out cold, but was stunned, his eyes rolled back into his head and feet twitching as he flopped down hard on the floor onto his huge hairy gut.

The manager stood slack-jawed and shrieked, "Is he dead?" He knew intuitively a dead customer in the lobby could affect his quarterly bonus.

Bailey intervened. "Perhaps I might be of some assistance." He calmly grabbed a handful of bum hair and a handful of pants around the bum's crotch, made fists and twisted, creating a painful scalp lift and atomic wedgie groin crush. The combination of pain compliance techniques caused cat dude to nearly levitate from the floor involuntarily and come out of his drug-induced... whatever that was.

As the street bum abruptly came to his senses, he squealed, "The N Dubya KGB will hear of this, you bastard!"

"The N Dubya KGB doesn't care about your white ass *or* mine, pal," Bailey huffed as he maneuvered the wiggling cat corpse collector towards the double glass doors. "Cat's have rights too, you wanker." Bailey knew from his former career that the best logic to use when debating bums is bum logic. It doesn't have to make sense. It just has to remain generally on topic and be stated loudest.

Bailey directed the cat bum terrorist, who squealed in pain as he moved on fingertips and tiptoes, to the door and out onto the sidewalk before releasing him.

Bailey watched the failed flying eye-ball-eater scurry away, disappearing down the street generally unharmed, like a captured hyena returned to the Serengeti after getting vaccinated by some do-gooder veterinarian or whatever it is they do on those dumb cable television nature shows. *The animal show network might get better ratings if they filmed street bums being released into the wild after getting bounced*, he thought.

No one else in the storage facility gave the matter any attention. They just stared at their phones. But they hadn't tried to assume the Bailey's place in line either. He returned from ejecting the bum and calmly approached the counter, careful not to step in any bum snot. He asked the manager, "Got any of that hand sanitizer they used to have everywhere?"

The manager snickered and produced a bottle of the once ubiquitous anti-germ lotion from behind the counter. "Help yourself, pal. Thanks for the assistance."

"No problem. Glad to be of some use for a change. To

be candid, I sort of enjoyed it," Bailey said with a crooked smile that the manager found to be surprisingly sincere and friendly considering he just gave a violent psycho the heave-ho moments before.

"You're pretty wiry for a, uh…," the manager paused, wanting to express respect and recognize, but not insult, the gentleman's age.

Bailey knew what the manager was trying to say and shrugged. "The secret is body mechanics, vodka, and Tylenol."

The manager smiled, uncertain if he was serious or kidding.

Bailey continued. "Maybe you can set me up with a couple of eight by twelves. I'm moving back here from Havasu. Downsizing. I need to store some stuff."

The manager frowned. "Sorry to hear that." He corrected himself, "Not sorry you are storing stuff with us, but sorry you are moving to Mesa. Havasu is nice. Why on earth are you coming back here of all places?"

"Wife passed. I have friends here, it's closer to the doctors and big hospitals, and airport for travel… I don't want to learn a new town. You get older, you think about that stuff."

The manager nodded in understanding. "Makes sense. Speaking of learning, where'd you learn that *bum rush* move, the Army?"

Bailey laughed. "Nah, I was a cop here. I retired many moons ago. He extended a hand. The name's Frank Bailey."

The clerk reached across the counter and shook it. "Welcome home, Mister Bailey. Let me get you your storage units."

"Thanks, pal. It's good to be home... I think."

***

Two months later, the move was complete, the home in Havasu sold, and it was time to do... what?

Bailey stood on the eighth-floor balcony of his new corner apartment, alone with his thoughts, sipping a cup of coffee as the sun broke over the Superstition Mountains to the East. *Renting was the right move. Why buy a place in this market,* he asked himself? *All I need is a two-bedroom joint, a place to sleep, and an office to pay bills from. Plus, this joint is modern, stylish and has a top of the line fully equipped gym I'll never use.*

He was paraphrasing the pitch from the rental agent, but the pitch was accurate. It was a spacious place with an amazing view.

His thoughts turned to next steps... What to do until he died? What to do next? Eventually, I'll have to do something with the cash from the sale of his place at the lake... but not today.

Real estate is annoying. Especially the paperwork.

Then the question... did I do the right thing coming back here? They say you shouldn't make any big decisions for a year after a spouse dies but how many years do I have left? Cops tend to check out early... like Denise did. And now I'm back here. I could have found a place in Hawaii or Florida.

He stared out to the city, remembering when there were no downtown apartment buildings, casting his mind back to the old days. A time when Mesa had wild weekend cruising down Main Street. Cars and pickup trucks were bumper to bumper from Extension to Pioneer Park. The sidewalks were packed. There were lots of hopping bars and restaurants of all types from creepy dives to upscale rooftop nightclubs. And people wandered around enjoying themselves as they were actually doing business in the local stores. Not that this new version of downtown was bad, it was just different. It looked deliberate now, a more structured attempt at being a local downtown rather than an organic real downtown with the generational local businesses with something *real* to do after five in the evening.

"Maybe I'm missing something. It might be me. I'm out of touch."

He took another sip from the heavy black and gold London Bridge tourist mug Denise gave him as a silly gift when she moved in with him.

Life was stabilizing here. It was time to write a new chapter.

But what kind of chapter is alone, old, aimless, and back where I started?

Living out of town for twenty some years, Bailey lost contact with most of his friends. He fretted over reconnecting. Getting together will feel awkward. What would there be to talk about? Who's alive and who is gone? Doctor visits? Pending surgeries? Sharing the tragedy of having to pee every half an hour? Getting old is bullshit. Old person conversations suck.

He looked west towards Country Club Drive.

"I wonder if the Florentine Room is still there?" he thought as he turned away from the glare of the morning sun.

But who wants to drink alone... or be seen drinking

alone?

His cell phone buzzed. He walked back to the kitchen counter where he left it and answered the call.

"Mister Bailey?"

"Yes."

"This is the Office of the Mayor. His honor would like you to come to his office tomorrow morning at nine. Can you be there?"

"Who is this really?"

The caller snickered. "Really. Mayor Henry James would like you to stop by. May I tell him yes?"

"Well, the Queen of England wanted me to stop by for tea, but I can juggle some things around. Sure, I'll be there."

"Sir, I believe the Queen expired."

"Never say *expired* to an old person."

Another snicker. "I'll tell him to expect you, sir."

The caller disconnected.

Bailey looked at the phone in his hand and said, "Office of the Mayor. I'll have to remind him I used to be his boss."

CHAPTER 2

City Hall

Bailey stood outside looking at the eight-story structure, remembering the old days. City Hall. At one time, the Special Investigations Unit occupied the entire second floor. It worked out better than anyone expected. Back then there was a delightful little diner facing the back parking lot area and there was a bank on the ground floor. The city owned the building but hadn't fully occupied the structure.

Now, it looks more like a fortress. Cold, unwelcoming, and lifeless.

Bailey went inside. The lobby was vast, empty, and void of any discernible character. There was a large receptionist area in the center of the room. To the side was a workstation near a waiting area. He saw a young man sitting behind a desk there.

He is either security, a police officer, or preparing to invade a small South American country. With the beards, soft uniforms, tattoos, and tactical vests, it's difficult to tell. Or maybe I'm just old and this is better. It's not for me to decide. These guys have a whole set of new problems that we never had to deal with.

The lady at the desk spoke, seemingly surprised to see a human life form in the lobby. "May I help you?"

"I'm here to see the mayor."

"Well, I'm afraid that's impossible," she stated dismissively with a smile that was as fake as a forty-dollar Nogales Rolex.

"No, it isn't."

The guard, cop, commando, whatever, menacingly rose from his chair and assumed a gunfighter stance.

Bailey slowly gave the receptionist his driver's license. "Please call him. He asked to see me. I'm a retired City of Mesa police lieutenant. We have an appointment."

I'm a nicely dressed, well-groomed, senior citizen with a three-thousand-dollar wristwatch. Why am I being treated like a damp turd on a dinner table?

She accepted the license like it was a dead rat. The officer, hearing the word lieutenant, sat back down.

Bailey grew impatient. *I don't think she believes me. At least that officer can figure out I'm not a troublemaker.*

The frowning lady made a call.

A few whispers were spoken into the phone, then she looked at Bailey. "Someone will be down to get you."

"I can't simply take the elevator up? I used to work in this building"

"It's security. We can't allow people to go into City Hall. At least not unescorted. It's quite risky. Homeland Security stuff," she said, again dismissively.

Sounds like bullshit stuff.

Bailey patiently waited by the elevator, glad to get away from the receptionist and the obviously bored officer. *I wonder who he pissed off to get stuck in this gig?*

Within a minute, the elevator doors opened, and a young man greeted him. "Lieutenant Bailey, the Mayor has told us so much about you. Welcome." Two people stepped off the elevator car at the same time as the young man. A tall woman and a short, stocky man. Their eyes were deader than Caitlyn's pecker. Bailey felt a cold tingle down his spine. All his cop senses were telling him something. But what?

Bailey ignored them and shook the young man's hand. Finally, a normal, nice human being.

Aboard the elevator, Bailey patiently watched the floor numbers change on the digital display, unaware of the turn his life was about to take.

The Proposition

To an outsider looking in, the two men might have been negotiating a public works contract. One, clearly the man in charge, in an expensive tailored dark blue wool suit, the other in a subtle dark gray plaid sport coat, black polo, black slacks, and black Johnson and Murphy loafers. But the meeting was a reunion rather than business. Mayor Henry *Hank* James had a proposition, an idea that required a miracle. He needed to convince his old partner Frank Bailey to willingly volunteer for a special job. A job for which he was uniquely unqualified.

Bailey stood at the window, taking in the expansive view of the city. "Henry, it seems like yesterday we were working patrol out there together. I can't believe the citizenry elected your dumbass mayor, Henry."

The skinny, balding former police lieutenant and the chunkier gray-haired former assistant chief-turned-mayor were alone in the 8th floor executive conference room of city hall, gazing out together at the city they once protected together.

The mayor smiled wistfully and adjusted his tie before replying. "I wish you'd still just call me Hank, brother.

For some reason, the press started this Henry, or Mayor Henry businesses, or whatever the hell it is, and it sort of caught on."

"I hate the press."

"Everybody does," Henry replied as solemnly as a prayer.

Bailey asked, "So, why are we here rather than meeting at the FOP Lodge?"

"Sit down, Frank. Quit being so paranoid."

"I'm not paranoid. This is City Hall. I'm wary... nothing good ever comes out of this place for a cop, even a retired one."

A mouse-quiet assistant came into the room and delivered a coffee service and a tray of donuts, poured out two cups, and then disappeared out the door, leaving the two men in privacy.

Bailey took a sip of coffee, then asked, "So, how long have you been a disgusting two-bit piece of crap political hack, Henry?"

Hank snorted a laugh. "It's nice to talk to someone who isn't kissing my ass for a change. It's been too long since I spent time with someone who didn't want something. Someone I can trust."

"If you trust me, you have no business being the mayor for a city of over half-a-million people," Bailey said with a slight grin. "Seriously, how long has it been?"

"Two terms to the council and three terms as mayor, Frank. I can't believe it either. But I'm done now. Tomorrow it's all over."

Bailey parked himself in one of the tall dark red leather chairs across from Henry and leaned back, making himself comfortable. "I liked you better when you were a cop."

"*I* liked me better when I was a cop. Speaking of cops, did you hear anything about a skinny old guy assaulting someone in a storage locker facility? I guess he threw him into the street like a bouncer or maybe a retired cop." Hank's expression changed to that of a kid who found a nickel in his pocket.

Shit.

"Sounds like crazy talk, Hank." Bailey's brain went into high gear. Where is he going with this? Bailey tried to appear unconcerned. I worked undercover for many years. I know how to act unconcerned. But Hank worked undercover with me, and he knows how to tell if I am faking a lack of concern. Shit.

Hank continued, "Yeah, the guy making the report was nuts. He became agitated and ending up fighting the cops. The storage locker manager said he didn't see anything like that happen though." *I dodged a bullet. I owe you one, manager guy.*

"So, case closed." Bailey said, hoping the case was closed.

"Yeah, the guy's in county psychiatric now. You know, he hit one of our officers with a dead cat. He was carrying it concealed. Which, as it turns out, isn't a crime. For some reason I thought carrying a conceal cat was some kind of crime, but if it's dead, it's legal. Anyway, that's something you don't see every day. He's nuts, but even crazy people tell the truth sometimes."

Hank drilled Bailey with his eyes.

Is that an amused or accusing look? I can't tell. Bailey quickly changed the subject. "So, what's next for you,

Mister Mayor?"

"The wife and I are moving to Corpus Cristi. And after we move, I won't be able to help you, so don't even bother asking," the mayor said almost dismissively.

"Wait… Help me what?" Bailey asked with an edge of concern in his voice.

The mayor broke eye contact and looked out the window over the city. "With your, uh, new appointment… to the uh, citizen review board."

Bailey came out of his chair, agitated and confused. "The what? Are you mental? What would I do on the citizen review board? I'm out of all that crap. I'm here to get drunker than a Canadian snowbird and hopefully… eventually… die or something… or whatever fully retired people do. I'm not a politician."

"I'm not asking you to be a politician."

"I've been retired for almost as long as I was a cop. I've been doing boat deck wash-downs part-time for the past four or five years. Why don't you ask me to do some boat deck wash-down advising? I'd be qualified to do that. I'm not a cop anymore, bud."

Hank raised the palm of peace and tried to de-escalate. They both sat down. "Calm down. Hear me out. Just try to be agreeable for once."

Bailey wasn't inclined to be agreeable, rather, he became highly agitated. He leaned across the table and barked, "Hear out what? I don't want to hear *anything* out!"

Hank leaned in, too. He ignored the outrage and persisted. His next words were measured and carefully spaced. "Just drink your cup of free city coffee and eat those free city donuts." Then suddenly, his voice jumped in volume, command tenor, and pitch, "And shut your disrespectful pie hole, Lieutenant. I'll tell you *what* and you'll damn well listen."

Bailey stood, came to a somewhat pathetic position of attention, shut his pie hole, and calmed down as directed. He might be retired, but he still knew when to follow orders. He might have been Hank's boss twenty-five years ago, but this was the mayor he was talking to, and a man with a far more successful career than his.

Hank didn't let him off the hook right away. He gave him the full ten-second boss stare before speaking. "Thank you. Now sit down."

"But, uh..." Bailey resettled into his chair, not totally ready to allow his former partner to state his case. "I haven't been a lieutenant for twenty-five years, and when I was, you were a sergeant..."

"So," Hank frowned.

Bailey pressed, confused but fairly certain he had a point to make. "So, I don't know... I don't think you are allowed to give me orders. I think I can still give you orders, or something... because of time... I don't know... or uh, science."

The mayor sighed a resigned sigh as both men sat across from each other at an impasse, "Do you want to hear *what* or not?"

Still grumbling, Bailey calmed down a bit more. "Fine. Give me the *what*. He stared Hank in the eyes as he took a giant bite out of his donut while snatching another gut bomb from the silver serving tray like a petty thief. He was pissed off, but he still really was a cop at heart. A donut is a donut. *Cop Crack*. At least in the old days.

Mayor Henry took a deep breath, gathered his thoughts, made a grim mayor face, then continued. "The new incoming mayor is a liberal anti-cop pussy. I don't trust him. He's sketchy as hell. The city council is a pack of *defund the police* commies. The citizen review board is stuffed with cop-hating weirdos and beatnik knobs. I have one appointment I can make to the Review Board as mayor and it's a permanent position. The new mayor can't kick you off. Nobody can kick you off. You'd be bulletproof."

"No thanks." Bailey talked while annoyingly munching on a mouthful of donut. "Sounds like a bullshit job with a bunch of bullshit jerks who do bullshit things for bullshit reasons. Not interested." He punctuated his refusal with an unnecessarily loud slurp of delicious free city coffee.

Henry, known as being calm in chaos, was uncharacteristically perturbed. "Just for once, shut the hell up and listen to me, dumbass. You still love the PD, and I do too. The cops are taking a beating in the press, politics, and the courts... They have nobody to back them up. My last big middle finger to these weasels is to appoint you to that board position. Think about it, you can do ride-alongs whenever you want, go into any precinct any time you want, make all of the new guys listen to your stupid stories, and argue with dipshit commies to your heart's content. And here is the best part. You get fifty thousand dollars a year to do it."

The intentionally obnoxious donut chewing stopped as his jaw dropped.

"Fifty thousand?" Bailey perked up a bit, his chin tucked and turned towards his shoulder and his eyebrows perked. He was listening.

"Yep, it's a paid position. Like a professor emeritus with guaranteed eternal funding."

Bailey took a moment and then leaned back in his chair. His facial expression changing from surprise to that of a poker player holding a full house. "Did you forget I inherited some cash before I retired? I'm doing okay with that money and my pension. I got some other investments, too. Plus, Denise had a generous insurance policy when she passed. I'm not a rich man in the scheme of things, but I'm rich for a retired cop."

"Do you have *fuck you* money?"

"No, but I do have *go piss up a rope* money."

"Yeah, I know, but that extra four grand a month or so could pay off your bar tabs."

"I don't drink anymore."

"You don't drink any less."

"Point taken."

"Listen, Frank. I know this has been a hard year for you. Hell, the past two or three years since your wife became ill. You need something to do. Something important. This could be it. A few hours a week. Just give it a shot. They can't fire you, but you can resign any time you want if this thing gets to be too much. Just take it. Get paid to be a dickhead instead of doing it for free. They give you the title of Commissioner."

"I prefer Lieutenant."

"You can be either one."

"I'm not interested."

"You can be a voice for the troops. You'd love it."

"So, you're saying I will get fifty thousand a year to be a voice for the street cops *and* be a total asshole?"

"Not a total asshole, just an above average asshole."

"And nobody can do anything about it?"

"By city charter, they have to let you do whatever you want, within the confines of the law. They made it official so *they* could screw the cops without interference. It's time we use that to our advantage."

"And I get paid?"

"Yeah. You get paid whether you do anything or not. So, do we walk down to the city clerk's office and make it official?" Hank produced a government-issued smile. He extended his hand in the internationally recognized 'deal closer' configuration used by the classical three 'C's' of making decisions against your own interests: Car salesmen, Con artists, and Congressmen.

Bailey remained motionless, staring ahead blankly for a full and uncomfortably long ten seconds, then reluctantly succumbed to Hank's will. "Deal."

Both men stood and shook hands.

"Welcome to the City of Mesa Citizen Advisory and Review Police Board, Frank. May you rain chaos upon their shitty little anti-cop parade." Hank's grin was genuine this time.

Bailey said to him, "Thanks for nothing, pal. So, what's next?"

"For you, nothing right now. I'll notify the board and send out an all-city personnel memo this afternoon." Hank's victory on the matter was short-lived as he remembered his other agenda item. Suddenly, his eyes started darting side to side as if he was about to reveal a secret or tell an outrageous lie. "Oh, and one other thing."

Bailey cautiously let go of the hand he was shaking and took a step back. "Yeah, what?"

Hank whispered in a conspiratorial tone. "Uh, do you remember when we got that obituary about Quintero out of Pittsburg about two years ago?"

Bailey softened at the mention of their old academy mate and partner on the street. "Yeah, of course. That was a shocker. I thought he'd live forever. We were quite a trio back in the old days, weren't we? Like brothers... until he went off the deep end with that whole puppet thing. Yet, he might have been the best undercover cop I ever worked with, crazier than a bedbug, but..."

Hank interrupted Bailey's reminiscing. "Uh, well, the thing *is*, he faked it."

"What?"

"Yeah, he's fine, totally not dead. It was another one of his weird hoax things. Pittsburg PD confirmed it after the city insurance department started an investigation into how to pay his death benefits after no claims were ever filed."

Bailey eye rolled, then grunt laughed. "That turd."

Hank grinned. "Yeah, classic Quintero."

Bailey's eyes suddenly widened. He framed his next question with a combination of fear and an accusation, like a vegan quizzing a waiter about beef in his grain bowl after already taking a bite. "Wait... Quintero's not *here*, is he? He's not back in Mesa?"

Hank's face swapped the smile for a deep frown. He whispered hoarsely like he was narrating a horror movie. "Nobody knows *where* he is. Quintero went completely off the grid again." Hank paused, leaned in, and added words that carried the essence of a threat. "He could be anyplace."

Bailey slumped. "Lord have mercy on us all."

CHAPTER 3

The Snag

The next morning, Bailey received another unexpected call. "Hello."

A woman's voice responded. "Yes, is this Mister Bailey?"

"Yes."

"This is Ms. Angora Pillsworth-Smith. My pronouns are she and her."

"Congratulations."

After an uncomfortably long pause and a loud throat clearing, the woman continued. "I am the *executive* secretary of Police Chief Howard Hinkley."

"Does the chief have pronouns too?" habitual wise-ass Bailey asked. He liked the mayor's secretary better than this condescending windbag.

Her voice became slightly more melodic and friendly, evidently missing the sarcasm. "Why yes, he does, thank you for asking. His pronouns are he and him. And he would like you to be his guest for breakfast as a *welcome* to the Citizen Review Board, if you haven't already eaten, of course. There will be a gluten-free and vegetarian menu, naturally."

"Naturally." Bailey suppressed a snicker.

She continued, "I'm terribly sorry about the short

notice. Will you be available?"

Bailey didn't believe this woman was terribly sorry, at all. He suspected this short notice was a power play intended to establish a pecking order.

She thinks she'll make the new kid leap through some hoops to meet the big dog. But why not play along?

Bailey decided to have some fun with the pretentious nitwit. "Fortunately, I *am* available she and her Angora. Look, I'm not up to speed on how all that pronoun bullshit works. May I just call you ma'am?"

Her voice tenor assumed the expected level of alarm and indignation. "Sir, *that* language is offensive."

"Well, just tell me where and when to meet the chief and I'll quit talking to you. Win-Win."

He could hear the exasperation in her tone as she breathlessly huffed out a reply. "The Clifton Cafe. It's at Dobson and Main. He can meet you there in an hour."

"Please tell him I'll be there. And I'm terribly sorry if I hurt your feelings. It must be awful for you being born so fragile. The world is so... *savage* nowadays," Bailey said, as he laid out a fat dose of faux concern.

"I believe we can let it go *this* time, Mister Bailey," she stated with utter condescension. "But please, in the future be more empathetic to the identity of our more vulnerable groups. We are *not* living in the dark ages. We are... *civilized* now, Mister Bailey. In spite of what *your* type might think, This isn't the eighties anymore, sir."

The woman disconnected abruptly.

He mimicked her last words. "It isn't the eighties anymore, sir." Bailey looked at his phone and smiled. "This is going to be so much fun... and the eighties *were* awesome, lady."

***

Bailey drove west on Main Street in his murdered-out black six-year-old Mercedes C300, windows down and the radio gently pouring some Miles Davis into the passenger cabin, he glanced down at his vintage Rolex Air King wristwatch. It was ten-till-nine.

Feeling sketchy today.

Bailey tried to remember what the chief looked like. He had seen photos before on the news. *If memory serves, the executive of the PD is an out-of-towner drafted into the city by that limp handshake of a mayor who preceded Hank. It seemed like this new chief was from Los Angeles or San Francisco... somewhere stupid... Not Tucson... or was it that guy? It doesn't matter.*

Bailey swerved to miss a transient stumbling out onto the street. His mind wandered as he closed in on a meeting he never really wanted to have.

If the word on the street is legit, this police chief hates cops more than he hates criminals, and he's more of a political ladder-climber than a crime fighter. I'm breaking bread with a typical modern big-city dipshit chief.

He maneuvered through moderate traffic and the annoying trolley lines. Right on schedule, Bailey pulled into the Clifton Cafe lot and found a parking spot. There was no one outside waiting for him, so perhaps the chief already went in and found a table.

Rude, but not unexpected. Another power play?

Bailey got out, locked the car, and walked in. Instinctively he entered the threshold and stepped to the left, out of the fatal funnel.

Never stand in a doorway collecting incoming lead.

He scanned the large dining room, looking for a man in uniform, while checking for exits, and eyeballing the place for potential threats. It's a habit that sticks with you. Instead, he spotted a pasty looking chubby turd in a mismatched coat and blazer waving at him from a corner table in the back. In front of him was a large plate of pancakes and bacon.

So much for the gluten-free and vegetarian bullshit.

Bailey walked with purpose back to the table. The fat boy didn't stand. He just put his hand out as he chewed the last of a mouthful of pancake.

What a slug. This is worse than I expected.

Bailey shook his hand while the chief finished chewing his food and swallowed.

The Chief of Police said to him, "Nice to meet you, Mister Bailey. Welcome back to Mesa and the Citizen Review Board."

"Thank you." Bailey pulled out a chair and sat down.

This clown is the epitome of bad manners. At least he chews with his mouth closed.

The chief said, "Mister Bailey, I just wanted to go over some guidelines with you and make sure you know your place in the scheme of things. Although, I have to admit, I was surprised to hear of this appointment. It usually goes to someone of significance in the local community." He stuffed another big forkful of pancake in his mouth, chewed three times, and swallowed.

The chief continued, "I'll arrange for a sergeant to take you on a one-hour ride-along every month if you wish; otherwise, I doubt if we see much of each other. I'm very busy. I set this meeting up as a professional courtesy, which I do for any new board member." He took a sip of coffee, then continued. "If you don't want to do ride-alongs," he paused to cut out a bite of pancake while shaking his head dismissively at the idea of a ride-along, "I can just have the *Patrol Division Update* newsletter sent to you once a month." This time he closed his eyes with a self-satisfied nod as if he just brought peace to a years long military conflict. "That should be fine. It would actually be better for everyone to do it that way. Then *you* won't be disrupting police business. *Neither* one of us wants that, right, Steve?"

Did he just call me by the wrong name on purpose? Fuck this guy, Bailey thought.

Bailey replied to him, "Chief, I appreciate you meeting me. I wanted to go over some guidelines for you, too."

The chief stopped chewing and said, "What? Guidelines? Uh... I don't think you understand."

Now he's talking with his mouth full. I knew it.

Bailey continued, "If I'm addressed at a formal meeting with fellow police officers or retirees, I'll be referred to by my rank. You may call me Commissioner, Lieutenant, or Lieutenant Bailey. Secondly, my appointment is permanent. I'm not going anywhere. I'll be here long after you are gone, pal. Third. I'm someone who spilled his blood for this city, so I suppose that makes me significant; therefore, a significant person *did* take this position. And fourth, I'll be taking a hard look at every policy you write, action you take, and *each and every* word that comes out of your disgusting pie hole. If you screw up, I'll be taking a chunk out of your fat, sorry ass. I'm taking this appointment seriously, mister.

The only thing I'm not taking seriously is you, you rude, condescending prick. I *am* Mesa PD. You're just another drifting bureaucrat opportunist."

The chief raised his hand, tried to swallow his pancakes, and voice an objection, but Bailey didn't give him a chance.

"Oh, and by the way, there isn't jack shit you can do about any of this. So, I'll require a liaison to be available to me *anytime* I want to come into *any* station or precinct, ride with the officers, or spend time with any detectives. I'll probably spend quite a bit of time with your undercover teams and SWAT as well."

The chief finally gagged down his food and spoke. "Wait... what? This isn't how *any* of this works."

Bailey stuck a finger in the chief's face. "I was briefed by the mayor, pal. This is *exactly* how this works. I am *oversight* personified. I will monitor you and report to the citizens of this town. My next stops will be the radio stations and newspapers to announce my plans. I need them to know I'll be available for open and transparent interviews anytime they wish. So, thanks for the meeting, asshole. I believe our business is concluded."

Bailey took a piece of bacon off the chief's plate and popped it in his mouth. "And this doesn't taste like vegan to me, you phony vegetarian pussy!"

The chief sputtered, "But...but... but...."

"No buts, have your secretary call me with the name of my liaison within four hours to set up a meeting. I'll need to brief whoever you send thoroughly. And if I don't like who you send, I'll replace them until you get it right. Try to find a ten-to-twenty-year night-shift patrol officer. Somebody who hates your guts will work fine... You have four hours."

Bailey got up, turned his back to the chief, and returned to his car. The smile on his face was so wide it almost hurt.

***

Thirty minutes later, Bailey was pouring a cup of coffee in the small, but functional, galley kitchen of his apartment when the phone rang. Bailey took the call and his coffee cup out on his balcony.

"What in the Sam Hell did you do to the chief, Frank?" Mayor Henry howled. "He just blew up my phone, crying about you getting all abusive, intimidating, and he said... you might have stolen a... piece of bacon? Seriously, you ate his damn bacon? His BACON? You don't just eat a man's bacon!"

There was an uncomfortable period of silence on the phone.

"Guilty."

A ten-second silence followed.

Henry broke hush and laughed. "Good work, man. That's the result I was hoping for. I'm still pissed off about the council and city manager saddling us with that turd. I hope you make his life miserable."

Bailey laughed. "Yeah, I have a feeling the two of us will never be close."

Henry's enthusiasm spilled. "Smart, Frank. You never want a venomous snake close. But good job, man. Keep him on his heels, and maybe that moron will resign. We can finally get a chief from *within* the department next time."

"No problem, brother. Oh, and before you leave town,

can you draft me a list of five or ten officers and sergeants I can trust? They're going to try to appoint a liaison to me, but I think I'll need to find my own guy."

"Will do, I've already been working on it. It's like the Dirty Dozen and you get to be Lee Marvin." Henry cackled. "Have fun, Frank. I almost wish I could stay and watch."

"Almost?" Bailey asked wryly.

"Yeah, exactly."

Hank disconnected. Bailey went back to his coffee and the view from the balcony.

Lee Marvin... yeah, I'll take that.

***

Bailey's phone rang again, exactly one minute before the four-hour deadline he set with the chief.

It's the charming secretary from the chief's office. She's fun.

An annoyingly self-satisfied voice came on the line. "Mister Bailey, this is *Mizzzz* Angora Pillsworth-Smith, the chief's *executive* secretary again. We have selected a liaison officer for you, as per protocol. You can meet them at the chief's office in one hour."

It occurred to Bailey that Mizzzz Angora Pillsworth-Smith's initials could also stand for Angry Piece of Shit.

Bailey tossed a lie at her. "No, I already found a liaison officer. I'll reach out to the chief with the name later. Did you have any other questions? I'm busy reviewing your job description."

Ms. Angora Pillsworth-Smith was flabbergasted, "What? Why I never..."

"Not even once? Sad."

She disconnected. Bailey envisioned her slamming her desk phone into the cradle. He smiled.

Bailey spoke to his city view. "I could get used to this 'board' thing."

There was a pleasant little ding sound on Bailey's phone indicating a text message with a note attachment had arrived. It was the list of officers from Mayor Henry.

Bailey walked back into the kitchen and retrieved the coffee pot. He took it out to the balcony, then went back to his office to gather his computer, his favorite vintage mechanical pencil, and a notepad.

He mumbled to himself, "This is going to take a while."

He settled into his favorite balcony chair, took a sip of coffee and enjoyed one more long gaze at the expansive city view to the north and west and of Superstition Mountain to the east, then began his review of the file with a quick read-through.

Number one: Officer Jones J. Jones. — Nickname — Jones. Young but experienced. Five years on the job. Five years on graveyard shift. Refuses any other shift, promotion, or specialty assignment. No known friends in the department. No known friends on the planet. Hobbies are rumored to be fast cars, fast motorcycles, and guns. Leads the department in arrests every month. Considered the best back-up in patrol division. He hates the chief.

Number two: Sergeant Harry Bell — Nickname Slay Bell — Fifteen-year Robbery Homicide detective sent to day shift patrol after sixth officer-involved shooting. Career total of eight shootings. Also, early in his career during a short hitch on the narcotics unit, he allegedly pushed a suspect off a balcony resulting in a fatality that fortunately, the grand jury chose not to indict him on. He hates the chief.

Number three: Detective Donna Fitzgerald Kennedy — Nickname Ma Donna or Madonna. Burglary Detective. Fifteen-years on the job. Married with four kids, so her attendance record isn't great. Like most burglary detectives, she is a walking encyclopedia and has the highest case closure rate and the highest property recovery rate in her division. The chief wants her back in patrol to teach her a lesson. She is hanging on to her job by a thread. She hates the chief's guts.

Number four: Sergeant Jim Bob Patch — Nickname Patch Man. Swing Shift patrol sergeant and chronic subject of internal affairs investigations and citizen complaints, but perhaps the most popular employee on the police department. He holds the record for excessive force allegations, attitude towards the public allegations, and insubordination cases. He survives because his squad has the best performance statistics in the history of the department, clever preemptory CYA maneuvers, popularity, and according to some, a guardian angel in city hall. He hates the chief.

And last but not least, number five: Edgewater F. Patterson — Nickname Gumby. He's a detective from the Special Crimes Unit. He's been undercover for eight years. He looks kind of like a nerd, but he's probably the best cop on the police department. It sounds crazy but some people say he can see the future. The chief wants to pull him out of Special Crimes and put him in Admin working on Accreditation. He hates the chief's guts more than anyone. He's been hiding from the brass for six months. It's a long story.

These guys are awesome. Bailey pondered the file. Phone numbers, badge numbers, immediate supervisors, everything he needed was all there. He was fascinated with number five. *We had a guy just like that back when I was in command of Special Crimes in '89. Eerie. Perhaps these Nostradamus cops are like witch doctors or something, weaving through space and time, hiding within the ranks, protecting law enforcement from evil spirits. Shit! Maybe it's the same guy. Maybe he's a time-traveler. That would explain the see-the-future business.*

Bailey sighed. *No one is more superstitious than cops. No one is more conspiracy theory oriented than cops... get a grip, Frank.*

Bailey went back into the kitchen and retrieved a short dog of Jack Daniels from the cabinet. He dosed his coffee, then put the little bottle back in the cabinet. *This is the only known repellent for cop voodoo. I have no choice.*

Another ding

Bailey read one more note from Henry, a new follow-up message. It read: Bonus name for you, Bill Spooner, Deputy Chief, he should have been chief. The current chief hates him and is trying to force him to retire. Bill is a cop's cop. He's honest, but he won't make waves when he needs to. He's too much by the book. If he could learn to bend the rules just a little bit, he could be one of the great ones. You can trust him. That's it for now. Good luck. Henry

Bailey thought about it. *Spooner, I need to talk to him.* He scratched a quick note on his pad.

Getting back to work, he put all the contact information from the six names into his phone address application and then started on his calendar. He wanted to meet all these people, his people, the people he had been away from for far too long.

As he developed a schedule, his news app popped up with a notification in the corner of the screen, a breaking story. The headline was disturbing.

Fifth homeless person found dead in Mesa this year. Does the city have a serial killer?

CHAPTER 4

Bailey ate an early dinner and caught a nap. It had been a while since he had to stay awake all night. Catching a graveyard shift on patrol with Officer Jones J. Jones seemed like a good idea after the meeting with the chief, but now, at ten in the evening, not so much. If he fell asleep during what would probably be a boring eight hours, he'd never live it down. Word gets around at the police department, and it's always exaggerated.

If I doze off, the next day everyone in patrol division will be saying I died, and Jones had jump-started my ass with CPR. Shit. I'm so old I might really die.

A shower, fresh clothes, and a coffee didn't do much to create an energy surge either. *I'm usually in bed by nine. What was I thinking?*

Bailey checked himself in the mirror before leaving. He shrank a little from his original six-foot-two on the day he became a cop. His hair was mostly gone and what was left of it turned white. He was a skinny, wrinkled-up old man. But the black soft-leather dress shoes, black slacks, and charcoal gray Pima Cotton T-shirt with the navy blazer at least made him look more like a cop than a retirement home refugee. He checked again on the fit of the belt holster for his old Glock 26. The weapon and spare magazine didn't imprint, so, unless he told someone he was armed, no one would notice. Same with the fixed-blade knife taped upside-down on the back of his calf. Old habits die hard.

A message appeared on his phone: *out front.*

Bailey took a deep breath and headed for the door, slipping the leather sap, his lead filled leather strap, on the kitchen counter into his front pants pocket on the way out. *Old habits.*

Bailey saw the patrol car in the parking lot. It looked like it might be a low-rider or an overloaded vehicle. There was a planetary-sized mass of some type behind the wheel, possibly human.

Bailey walked to the passenger door, opened it, and leaned in. "Officer Jones?"

A voice from within grunted with urgency. "Hot traffic. Get in."

The voice was surprisingly deep. He sounds like the actor who did that 1950s movie about moonshiners, and the western... Robert Mitchell? No, that isn't it, but it's something like that. Bailey thought if he were a scientist instead of a retired cop, he might be able to calculate how this behemoth squeezed in behind the wheel of a car designed for human beings.

Bailey looked over his host for the evening. The officer's leather gear had a deep polish, not shiny, but oiled and buffed. To an old-school cop, that is the sign of professionalism. Most of the modern officers wore plastic and polyester gear. An old-timer knows that stuff will melt to your skin in a fire environment. Well cared for leather always looks good and will serve a lifetime if maintained. Obviously, this young man takes care of his gear.

Getting into a police car again, Bailey felt his heart accelerate for the first time in a long time that wasn't related to atrial fibrillation.

Officer Jones J. Jones gave Bailey a curious side glance as they sped out of the parking lot. Bailey caught it. He noticed Jones had green eyes, a rare characteristic in black people. In his case, the unique eye coloring provided a sinister look. However, his glance didn't seem malevolent, just curious. Bailey wasn't sure, but he felt like Jones wanted to ask something. He tried to break the ice by asking Jones something first.

"What do we have, Jones?"

"Knife fight. Six guys, Ranchero Bar. Broadway and Extension."

"Close," Bailey commented. "It's only a few blocks away."

Jones said to him. "I like knife fights." He said it so matter-of-factly, he could have been talking about sugar cookies.

How do you respond to that? "Yes, they're nice." *When in doubt, go with the flow.*

Jones hit the overheads, and they launched out of the parking lot and onto the street like a surface-to-air missile fired from a destroyer.

Bailey subconsciously cinched his seat belt. He said nervously, "When I was a cop, I taught pursuit driving. I love motorsports and high-performance vehicles."

Jones apparently shares these pleasures as well, only at a level that is either a felony, a sin, or a crime against humanity. I'm afraid to guess which.

Jones executed moves Bailey was pretty sure the car

was never designed for.

I don't know about the car, but I know I'm not designed for this shit! Scared shitless? Yes. Having the time of my life? Also, yes.

They hooked a hard right onto Broadway at sixty with two wheels off the ground. Bailey didn't think they would flip, because the force of Jones' weight on the driver's side was more powerful than any of those stupid laws of physics. The tires screamed like murder victims as Jones punched it hard, jamming the accelerator to the floor. Jones weaved through the light traffic, over a sidewalk to avoid a truck, clipped a garbage can, swerved back into the oncoming lane, and back into their own lane, never slowing down. They eliminated four blocks of traffic so fast that a wide-eyed Bailey didn't have time to squeal like a little girl, saving him some embarrassment. *Yeah, I haven't done that in a while,* Bailey thought.

As they closed within a half of a block of the Ranchero Bar, Bailey said, "I see the place. I'm pretty sure in my day, that building was a transmission shop."

The bar was about what one would expect to find on a knife fight call. A dump that was so dumpy, all the other dives in town were ashamed of it.

Bailey saw a group of assorted trucks and cars jammed into the parking lot that had somehow avoided their rightful place in a salvage crusher. Bailey began mentally noting his observations. *Six kids, three Hispanic, two black, and a white dude. I say kids, but they are all in their twenties or older.* Around them, the usual skank squad, screaming for the combatants to either stop, start, or get the hell out of there.

Bailey scanned the crowd for threats and problems.

He caught a glimpse of a man who looked vaguely familiar, but he didn't get a good look at him before he disappeared into the crowd. Then a young woman caught his attention. She had something in her arms. *Oh, that's a baby. I don't want to ever call a baby ugly, but I had to look twice to make sure it wasn't a possum.*

Jones grabbed his radio microphone. "We're going ninety-seven. One man down."

On the pavement was a seventh individual, another white guy. Bailey said, "I don't think that one on the ground is good at knife fighting, Jones. He's looking pretty dead."

Every one of the combatants who were still on their feet continued fighting like it was the last stand at Thermopylae, but with a bunch of local assholes rather than trained Greek and Persian soldiers. It wasn't pretty. Bailey noticed there were no clear sides either, it appeared it was every man for himself. Or at least every man and the occasional woman who would jump in, punch someone, then jump back out of the melee and back into the crowd.

Bailey's observations were interrupted by Jones twisting the wheel and pumping the brakes as the vehicle suddenly lurched like a spaceship re-entering the atmosphere. They skidded into the crowd perfectly.

THUMP.

The right front fender kissed the ass-end of one of the Mexican fighters, launching him into the side of the bar like a coyote in a cartoon.

One down, Bailey thought.

Jones looked at Bailey. "You should remain in the car, sir."

"Fuck that."

Jones either smiled or had a toothache. Bailey couldn't tell which. It only lasted an instant. Then, in the immortal words of one of America's greatest heroes, Jones growled, "Let's roll."

The three hundred or so odd pounds of cop mountain simply vanished out of the car in the blink of an eye. Before he could open his car door, Bailey looked out the windshield in time to see Jones punt one of the fighters up through imaginary goal posts to a meeting with Jesus. That one slowly slid down the wall like damp snot and landed on the guy who was hit by the fender, making a nice little stack of assholes. Bailey jumped out, slipped his sap out of his pocket, and went to work.

The sap, a stitched flat leather strap that has lead pellets inside, had been with Bailey for decades. It's a near-invisible equalizer and probably illegal. He held it in the palm of his hand.

A white guy approached him, hostile, big, and mean. "What the fuck are you going to do, old man?"

"I was just going to tell you, don't step in that dog shit." Bailey gave his sincere *dog shit warning* face.

The dumbass looked down.

Bailey swung wide and fast with the sap in his open hand, clocking the man with a solid slap on the left side of his head near the temple. The man's legs turned to spaghetti. He went down before he could tell Bailey he was mistaken about any dog shit being on the ground. Bailey's poetic side thought metaphorically, *well, there's some there now.*

Bailey sneaked another peak at Jones. At around six-foot-six, Jones was a lot more agile than Bailey expected he would be. There were only three armed felons left. Jones did a spinning back fist to number one, an elbow strike to the head on number two, and a spinning back kick to the side of number three's knee, all in under four seconds. The knee strike made an awful sound of bone snapping and tendons ripping followed by a visceral scream that couldn't have been any more soul wrenching if Jones had bayoneted the dude in the guts.

Jones yelled, "Get the zip ties out of the trunk."

As Bailey turned to retrieve them, a new guy burst out of the crowd and stabbed Jones in the meaty part of his left shoulder with a small folding pocketknife. Bailey drew his Glock, lined the assailant's head up in the front site, and prepared to smoke him.

Jones calmly gave Bailey the 'not now' look. Jones turned around slowly and deliberately, as the man stood frozen, surprised his knife had no effect. Jones smacked him in the center of his ugly mug with a blindingly fast right overhand lead punch that flattened the man's kisser as if he'd used his face to block a manhole cover shot out of a cannon. The assailant swayed for a moment, then dropped to the ground like a big wet turd through the bottom of a thin paper bag. Jones yanked the little knife out of his shoulder, folded it, put it in his pocket, and went back to work cuffing suspects.

The lady with Possum Baby approached Bailey. She was a red head with freckles, a few teeth, and apparently a meth habit.

"Who in the hell are you supposed to be?" she asked angrily.

Bailey suspected she was Mister Dog Shit's date for the evening. He resisted the urge to call her Possum Mama.

Bailey was a cop long enough to know that all stereotypes are real, cops just don't say that out loud. He guessed she was Irish-Catholic, so he went with an authority figure. "Vatican security, ma'am. The name's Brannigan. I'm here on a fact-finding mission."

"Oh shit!" She did three quick signs of the cross and a curtsey. "Will you bless my baby, Father Brannigan?"

Father? I might as well go with it. "And what is this, uh, lovely baby's name, my child?"

She spoke as clearly and formally as she could manage with her tongue piercing and missing teeth. "Francis Marsupial Johnson," your grace.

"Marsupial?" *What are the odds?*

She nodded proudly. "Yes, father. His baby daddy says it's Croatian for *Shining Star.*"

For all I know, it might be. "I believe that's correct, my daughter." Bailey put his hand on Possum Baby's head. "Ad nauseam, ex-post facto, quid-pro-quo, corpus delicious, et cetera, et cetera, be in the grace of God."

"Thank you, Father."

"Call me Frank."

"Thank you, Father Frank."

Bailey excused himself, retrieved the zip ties, and helped Jones secure the prisoners as every available cop in the city began rolling into the parking lot code three. Possum Momma faded back into the crowd, chatting up anyone who would listen to her about meeting Father Brannigan from the Vatican.

As a mob of badges began stringing yellow tape, dragging suspects to backseats, and taking names of witnesses, Jones pulled Bailey aside. "I might have accidentally caught you on my body cam knocking out that turd."

"Body cam?" Bailey asked. "We didn't have those in my day, thank God."

"Yeah, we all gotta wear them now, lieutenant."

"Oh, yeah? So, is that a problem?"

"Yeah. It's a problem. I got the word. The mayor, the chief, and all them candy-assed brass pricks are pissed off about you being back in Mesa and on the board. So, anything they can hang on you, they will."

"That was quick."

Jones focused on the camera problem. "Just say, you misunderstood my instructions to stay in the car... no wait, *you* thought *I* was in trouble, that guy assaulted you *before* I picked up what happened on the cam, and you were just pushing him away and he, uh... just fell. Self-defense."

"You good with that?"

"If you don't rat me out for getting stabbed."

"You're not reporting getting stabbed?"

"Camera didn't pick it up. I'd get benched for a month of evaluation and counseling. I hate evaluation and counseling. I got shot last month and didn't report it. I just fix this shit at home and keep it to myself, stay on the front line. It's better for everybody."

"Everybody?"

"The real cops."

"And you trust *me* with this information?"

"Are you the *real* Frank Bailey. The old SIU Lieutenant?"

"Yeah."

"You once shot a guy in the nuts who beat up an old lady and stole her purse on Main Street?"

"It might have been on Mesa Drive. Who remembers that kind of thing?"

They say you killed the chief, then retired... a real *dickhead* chief."

"I didn't *kill* him. We just had words, then later he had a heart attack. It was really not my fault."

"But you *did* kill him, didn't you?"

"Of course not!"

"Smart. No statute of limitations on murder. I'll keep my mouth shut."

"You don't have to, Jones. He just died."

"*Right.*"

"Whatever."

Jones said to Bailey, "Look. The real cops on this department are under siege, sir. That new chief they brought in from out of town is a dirty, scum-sucking, communist out to defund the police. He hates cops. Just like that chief did back in your day."

"Right." Bailey wasn't sure where this conversation was going.

"So, bottom line. You are like our messiah, here to save us with your position on that board. You got our back. We got your back."

"Messiah? That's a bit blasphemous."

"You're right... Uh, you're our Moses. yeah, Blue Moses... that's a good code name for you."

"I need a code name?"

"Yeah. Once you see how the anti-cop crowd works, you will definitely need a code name."

"And blue?"

"PD blue."

"Isn't that somewhat offensive in some way to somebody somewhere... or something?"

"No. The original Moses was like a cop. He had laws that he carried around in a big box. He wandered around in his beat aimlessly for forty years enforcing those laws. He carried a big wooden stick and wasn't afraid to use it. It's all in the Good Book. You are Blue Moses and you're going to lead our cops to the promised land... because *you're* here now, we're going to be able to do *real* police work again."

Bailey decided it might be wise to avoid arguing religious-based nicknames with a wounded bull moose who has anger issues. "Fine, Blue Moses it is."

Jones continued in a conspiratorial whisper, "And we keep this on the downlow, lieutenant. You know how rumors, innuendos, and accusations spread like wildfire in the police department. Before long, people start spreading around all kinds of crazy shit. We have to make sure we know who to trust as we save the department."

"Agreed. I know rumors go crazy at the PD. Mostly false, but they do go crazy." Bailey thought, *I wonder what he means when he says save the department. He sounds like Henry. Save it how?*

Jones calmed down from being a rage beast as quickly as he amped up. He softened his tone to a more human-like voice than Bailey had heard from him before now. Jones said, "Look, I don't have any friends, Lieutenant. I prefer it that way so I can keep to myself. I like operating alone. But I saw you ready to take out that little backstabber tonight. You didn't know me. You aren't sworn. It would have been your ass if you had shot somebody. But you were ready to shoot his dumb ass anyway. That took some balls."

"I'll never let a cop go down if I can stop it, Jones. No matter what."

"I believe you. And believe me when I say, I told you I ain't got any friends, but that changed. I got one friend."

"Yeah, brother. You do. I got your back, come hell or high water. It's the old way."

A forearm bump ended the conversation. The pair went back to work.

Two hours later, Bailey and Jones were sipping coffee and writing reports in a south Country Club Drive diner. Jones wasn't planning to have a meal, but he felt hypoglycemic, so he ordered a dozen pancakes for a snack. Bailey finished his witness statement carefully leaving out his knock-out slap and reframing it in a way that was mostly truthful, but not quite as epic. He just put his hands up to protect himself and the guy must have slipped and hit his head.

Jones heard a beep and checked his phone. He received a text message. "Lieutenant, that dead guy... fire got him to the hospital in time, and the surgeons brought him back."

"Great. So, it's not a homicide. That's good. He looked dead to me."

"I thought so too. It looks like it was close as it gets, but they saved him."

"He might have been a maggot, but he didn't deserve

to die in a parking lot like that. I'm calling it good news."

Jones agreed. "Me too." Jones stared at Bailey as he finished eating his last pancake like something was on his mind.

Bailey was perplexed. "What?"

"Why was that red-headed meth lady running around chatting up everyone at the scene and pointing at you? I saw you talk to her after clocking her boyfriend. Is she going to report us for something?"

"I don't think so. She just thanked me for my service and asked for the battered women's shelter number. I told her to call the front desk. We're good," Bailey said, uncomfortable with lying to Jones, yet understanding it was best if Jones didn't know the truth, in the event internal affairs ever got involved.

Jones was satisfied. "Good. I hope that's the end of it."

"I'm sure we'll never hear of it again."

Residence of Former Mayor Henry Jones - Texas

Henry and his wife were enjoying dinner at the end of their first full day of retirement at their new home. She asked, "So, have you heard anything on Frank yet?"

"Oh, he's just wreaking havoc. Like I expected."

"I'm surprised he did it."

Henry laughed. "I'm not. Between his ego and competitiveness, I can talk him into anything and make him think it was his idea."

His wife smiled. "Is that anyway to treat your best friend?"

"It was either get him involved in something or let him wind up alone with nothing to do. The old cold, blue darkness. You know what happens."

"We lost too many old friends because there wasn't anyone there to listen. Once hope is lost, all is lost. It breaks my heart. Do you think Frank was heading down the road to ending it all, Hank?"

"I want to live the time I have left never feeling like I need to worry about it again. Besides, only Frank can save the soul of the police department now."

They toasted to that sentiment.

She said, "So, you can save the city, the PD, *and* your old partner while you just relax, eating dinner with the most beautiful woman in town? Smart guy. No wonder you became Mayor and he wound up as a boat bum on the lake."

Henry grinned. "I was smart enough to marry you, oh wise one."

Police Headquarters the following morning

At 9:00 AM, the Central Precinct watch commander, Lieutenant Gabe Faller, was comfortably relaxing at his desk, reading a few travel brochures, planning his vacation, and enjoying his second cup of coffee when his intercom buzzed. He picked up the line and responded, "What is it?"

"Problem in the lobby, sir."

"What kind of problem?" he asked, a bit annoyed. Having a problem in the lobby this early on a Wednesday morning was unusual. He didn't join the police department to deal with anything unusual. Avoiding problems to get to the pension was his sole career objective. Everything else was a distraction.

"A bunch of women with babies," the desk clerk said, not thrilled with saying more than she had to with the notorious rat bastard lieutenant. He'd cut his own mother's throat to improve his position in the city. Engaging with him in any way was widely known as dangerous.

He wasn't sure he heard her correctly. Most of these civilian-employee half-wits talk like they have rocks in their mouths. "What? What do they want? Is this some pro-life protest group? Speak up."

She answered cautiously. "No... but they are Catholics."

Faller calculated the odds of deferring this until the next shift. No, it's impossible to push this back seven more hours. "Right, so... uh, well, other than a pro-life protest, what the hell else would they want?"

"Father Brannigan, sir. They want Father Brannigan."

"Who?"

"The Vatican Inspector assigned here to investigate bars, hotels, and I think gas stations? Maybe it's truck stops. I'm not really sure. There are a lot of versions of this being discussed in the lobby. But these women seem to know all about it."

"What?"

She added more pain to the discussion. "The media is here too, sir."

The watch commander gobbled some antacids from his desk drawer. "And... what? What do they want? The media? Why?"

Faller couldn't see anything good coming of this situation. Who can I blame this on?

"Sir, please come down here. It's getting out of control. A lot of these women are pretty sketchy."

The watch commander pushed a button on his computer to bring up the lobby surveillance cameras on his screen. There were over a hundred people crushed together in there. The place was packed with meth-mommas, normal mommas, pregnant women, babies, reporters, and the usual lobby slugs wandering around with a report in their mitts wanting something from someone. Some of the reporters seemed to be part of a television crew.

"Shit," he swore as he pointed at a man in the crowd. "That mother fucker is a news cameraman!"

He ran down to the tele-serve desk behind the plexiglass screens and found the civilian employee who called him. "What the hell is going on over here? Who is this Father Brannigan guy?"

"Evidently, he's been sent here from the Vatican on a top-secret joint task force operation. They say he performed a miracle last night. There was a baby stabbed or shot, something like that, and he brought him back from the dead. I never heard about any of this, Lieutenant, and I'm a Catholic. We must have ten pages of calls backed up wanting blessings, last rites, weddings, and a request for an exorcism that I'm pretty sure came from one of our jailers." She paused. "That jail one might be legit. There was some weird shit going on down there last night, sir."

One of the other front desk clerks piped in, "There's weird shit going on down there every night, sir. Thank goodness we have Father Brannigan now." He did a sign of the cross as punctuation to his comment.

The watch commander sputtered, "What? Exorcism in the jail? Back from the dead? Task force?" The watch commander started to panic. He was up for a full Commander position, third on the list. With pending retirements, he could make it by spring. So, why wasn't he briefed on any of this? Was he getting passed over? Was he out of favor? Did he waste his time sucking up to the chief for the past three years? And who the fuck is Father Brannigan?

The television news crew pushed their way to the front and pressed a camera against the plexiglass. There was no place to hide. A hot chick with a microphone started yelling questions, but the watch commander couldn't hear her. He wondered if this is how aquarium fish feel when you talk to them.

The civilian desk clerk hit a microphone button, and the news crew's voices could finally be heard.

The reporter shouted questions. "What is the status of the Special Vatican Task Force? Where is Father Brannigan? When did the chief authorize this project? What is the status of Operation Shining Star?"

The watch commander, who skillfully made the rank of lieutenant without ever making a real arrest, leaned over and puked in the wastebasket. Then, two of the female civilians at the front desk, one of whom was pregnant, also puked. The pregnant one couldn't stop puking. One of the male civilians started puking too. The one functional male front desk clerk, an old, retired patrol sergeant and former Marine named Paul Springfeld, who only took the job to supplement his pension for hunting trips, called for an ambulance, then casually strolled away, disappeared behind a structural pillar down the corridor, just outside the view of the hallway cameras, reached around, and pulled a fire alarm.

He waited a couple of seconds until the power automatically switched to the generator, temporarily resetting the cameras, then went back to the desk and tossed his ID card on the counter. "I've heard enough of this bullshit. I quit! Father Brannigan my ass. You bunch of dipshit pussies."

At that exact moment, Paul decided to sell his house and move to Costa Rica where he would fully retire. At least there, if people were going to be stupid, he wouldn't understand what they were talking about anyway. Semper Fi!

The Chief's Conference Room

In the chief's conference room, the fire alarm caused only a bit of concern at first, but not enough that anyone paid much attention to it until the emergency evacuation was announced over the PA.

The chief and his command staff scurried to the street facing window like a posse of lemmings.

"What the hell is going on out there?" a random deputy chief squawked as an ambulance rolled up in front of the building to haul away an employee.

Then, three fire engines pulled up with firefighters dragging equipment *into* the lobby, as about one-hundred or more women with babies swarmed *out* the lobby onto the front parking lot along with a television news crew and other various reporters, crowding around the firetrucks and impeding the firefighters. A dozen patrol cars began rolling in from the street to control the crowd but only added to the chaos. Yelling at pregnant ladies and ladies with babies was not going to get them to move, and it looked bad for the news cameras, so the officers simply joined the crowd, curious as to the veracity of the now rapidly spreading *hell demons being confined in the jail* story. Cops are particularly superstitious, and any supernatural event gets the benefit of the doubt.

A Homicide lieutenant who was busy flirting with the assistant chief's secretary wandered into the command group at the window and joined the conversation with his latest tidbit of news. "Something about an exorcism in the jail is what I heard. A demon possessed a crack-head then got a jailer too."

Some of the command staff responded with wide eyes. This detective lieutenant was known to be a hell of a cop. If he suspected demons, then there might really be demons in the jail. Even command cops are superstitious. The trait doesn't fade with rank or experience.

The chief did a double take. "A what?"

"Just saying, sir. That's what I was told."

Miss Pillsworth-Smith came jogging out, her flab wiggling as her speed-waddle brought her to the chief's side. "It's the Vatican Task Force, sir. They're in town. I wasn't told!"

The chief's face contorted. "The Vatican what?"

Pillsworth-Smith continued. "It's on the television news now. The Vatican Task Force is here, undercover, running an investigation. One of them saved a baby last night. Evidently, someone is on their way now from Rome to verify a miracle occurred. It's all I know so far that is completely confirmed by the news."

"Investigating what?" the chief asked, now needing to pee, and soon. Stress affected his bladder function.

Pillsworth-Smith whispered, "No one knows. But they think it has something to do with the police department."

The chief palm slapped his forehead. "Shit!"

Like a Greek Chorus, the rest of the command staff piped in with a supporting, "Oh shit," with the exception of veteran Mesa Deputy Chief Bill Spooner, who smiled. He thought to himself, *Edgewater Patterson's prophecy is coming true. Blue Moses has arrived to lead us to the promised land.*

***

In the reception area outside the conference room, a lone, old man with a visitor pass was waiting to see the Chief about a new community program. He quietly stood up and left the building, his floppy hat and jacket collar concealing his smile.

Bailey's Apartment

Bailey woke up at noon, his body sorer than he expected after the ride-along with Officer Jones J. Jones. He decided to wait a day or so before suiting up again and going out with the next officer on his list. He ordered a tube of heat liniment to be delivered from an online retailer.

Tonight is television, pizza, and beer.

Bailey made coffee, then flopped onto the couch, snatched the remote, and turned on the noon news. Another homeless person murdered in Mesa, a woman. This killing was also in the central corridor. Homicide didn't release any details. *Smart move. Keep the details quiet. Reduce the copycat potential.*

Then a lady reporter came on with red letters flashing the words *breaking news.* She had some amazing cleavage which was a news story in itself. She gave her *determined reporter blowing the lid off a big story* face. Bailey turned the volume up. Maybe this breaking news had something to do with the homeless homicides.

The newscaster spoke breathlessly, "This is Cara Carter breaking an exclusive story for you this morning. In an utterly shocking turn of events, we've discovered the Vatican is conducting an undercover investigation called Operation Shining Star, led by the famous exorcist Father Brannigan. The investigation is underway now, right here in the East Valley. The target is unclear, but it might be the police department itself. Shocking news, viewers, but there's more... in unconfirmed reports we've learned that Father Brannigan allegedly brought a baby back from the dead. The child, who was reportedly the victim of a random gang shooting, was saved by Brannigan with the mere touching of hands. Then, Father Brannigan allegedly performed an exorcism in the city jail. Whether these two alleged incidents are connected is, as of yet, unproven. We do understand that Vatican authorities are sending a team to Mesa in order to confirm this miracle. Our reporters have concluded the police department is perhaps the target of the investigation since the Chief, Howard Hinkley, admits no knowledge of Operation Shining Star and is presently stonewalling our investigation."

Bailey was dumfounded. *Possum Baby wasn't dead. He was just ugly!*

The cleavage lady turned to her left, "Roll the clip please."

A shaky video appeared of the woman reporter shoving a microphone into the chief's face. "What do *you* know about Operation Shining Star, Chief Hinkley."

Hinkley began stammering. "What? I, uh... no comment. I, uh... there is a... uh."

"Where is Father Brannigan?"

"Who?"

"What happened in the jail. Why are you doing exorcisms in the Mesa City Jail?"

"What? No, of course not, there are no exorcisms in the jail. That's ridiculous. We don't believe in that crazy mumbo jumbo."

"So, you say Catholicism is a bunch of crazy mumbo jumbo?"

The chief got an *Oh shit, I stepped in it* look on his face. "No, not that. I mean. What that thing is, I meant to say, it never happened."

"If you can't say, chief, then who is in charge here? Who knows where Father Brannigan is? Who knows why he's doing an exorcism in your jail? How many exorcisms have been done in the jail? How many demons do you have in custody?" The reporter yelled in the chief's face like a vengeful prosecutor breaking a lying witness on the stand, "Why are you keeping demons in the Mesa city jail, sir, WHY?"

"What the hell are you talking about?" The flabbergasted chief asked in desperation, praying to hear any words that made sense.

The lady turned to the camera, "There you have it folks, Chief Hinkley denies Catholicism is a real thing, he denies he has demons in the city jail, and he denies knowing anything about the heroic Father Brannigan and Vatican Task Force. Who is really in charge at the Mesa Police Department? This is Cara Carter signing off from the City of Mesa. Back to you, Stoney."

Bailey hit the pause button on his remote and started

yelling at the TV. "What the hell, Possum Momma? Can't you keep your pie-hole shut? That's the last time I ever bless that butt-ugly kid of yours."

He got up and grabbed two beers out of the refrigerator and snatched a bottle of Jack Daniels off the counter as he made his way back to the couch. *It's early, but this is an emergency.*

He poured a drink

Who saw what happened with Possum Momma? I don't think Jones knows. Mister dog shit was out cold. How did this get so far out of control? It's the old axiom that people have said for centuries, if you want to get news out to the world fast, tell some nasty red-headed woman on meth.

Frank started writing a list in his notebook.

Plan for next six days

1. Grow beard to hide my face. That will take three days, maybe a week.
2. Buy some lightly tinted sunglasses that I can wear all the time, inside or outside to hide my eyes.

I might still have a pair of yellow lensed glasses from the boat.

3. Wear my fedora to conceal the shape of my head. I can wear it everywhere.

I'll tell everybody I always wore it everywhere.

4. Wear my nice long German raincoat all the time and conceal my build.

Maybe start speaking with a German accent. No, scratch that. People might think it's an Italian accent. I'm not good at accents.

5. *Get someone to darken what little hair I have left*

and the new beard just a bit.

I was going to do that anyway.

    6. Never speak of this again. They can't prove I'm Father Brannigan.

Bailey placed his pencil down and poured another drink, followed it with a long pull on the beer, then filled the glass with whiskey. He leaned back on the couch and finally allowed himself to laugh at the absurdity of modern police command, the media, and the gullibility of the public.

Only another cop would understand this, and I have to take this secret to the grave.

He took another long sip of beer and did a sign of the cross, just in case.

Besides, I'm a Presbyterian. How is this my fault?

Bailey decided the whiskey needed some ice and his meritorious service as a priest deserved a bologna, mustard, and cheese sandwich for lunch. *What problem can't beer, booze, and bologna solve?* He hopped up and went to his galley kitchen to attend to it.

In all likelihood, the Father Brannigan thing will die down in a few days. Things like this are usually short lived, right?

Right?

CHAPTER 5

Central Division Briefing

Sergeant Jim Bob Patch was in his office an hour before the 3:00 PM shift started, chatting on the phone with his former academy mate, Homicide detective, Ronny Cortez.

"So, Ronny, this dead bum thing. All of them have been in the central corridor and we're getting nothing. The news reported another one."

"Patch Man, I don't know what to tell you. For some reason, city hall put a lid on this thing. It's buttoned down tighter than a nun's girdle. We shouldn't even talk about it on the phone."

"Then meet me for coffee. Fill me in. We can catch whoever it is doing this shit. But my guys can't help if we don't know anything."

"Officially, I ain't telling you jack shit, Patch Man. But I will have coffee with you to *talk* about the old days. *Right?* Nothing else... *on the record*. Understand?"

"Fair enough. Let me get my turds in their cars and on the street, then I'll meet you at the Castaway on MacDonald and Main in three hours. We can sit outside while we still can enjoy the nice weather."

"See you then."

Patch disconnected and started working on shift assignments, but he couldn't let it go. *Sometimes we are our own worst enemy. Everything is a secret.*

Homicide

Ronny Cortez knew if anyone could do it, Patch could turn up a lead on the string of homeless homicides. No one had more street sources and more energy in the central corridor of the city than the Patch Man. But the chief ordered a complete lockdown on any information, claiming the decision came directly from the City Manager's office. *Why would the City Manager be making case decisions?*

Ronny began putting the day's files into his briefcase when his partner, Gil Sanborn, burst into his cubicle. "We have another one."

"No way... we just finished one."

"Congratulations, we went from once a year to once a month, and now we're at a daily murder by this perp."

"That's bad, Gil. Real bad."

"No shit. I wish we had Father Brannigan with us on this one."

"Who?"

"The Vatican cop who's supposed to be in town. He's the best in the world. He found most of the Nazis who escaped after World War II and blew the lid off that Russian spy ring in France or someplace. Maybe England. One of those."

"That's news to me. Where did you hear all this?"

"Well, Father Brannigan was on the TV news and the guys in the gym were talking about it."

"I don't follow the news."

"Dude, if you don't follow the news, how will you know what's going on in the world? You have to be knowledgeable, man, if you want to be respected."

"I hate the news."

"You're a lost cause, Ronny. That's probably why you're single. At least *I* can hold an intelligent conversation on current events. Chicks dig an intellectual."

"Right."

On the way to the scene, Ronny surreptitiously texted Patch the code for a dead body call while Gil drove. *903 in alley, zero block S. Robson.*

The detectives found the crime scene perimeter being established by patrol officers with tape and the flashing lights of patrol cars. As per protocol with the string of homeless killings, a wider area than normal was being set up, and any visual was blocked by a forensic truck and the huge mobile command post vehicle.

Ronny worked his way through the perimeter and saw the dead body. It was jammed awkwardly between a dumpster and the back of the building. Dead bodies are difficult to handle; the dumpster was full. *Maybe more than one perp?* The deceased appeared to be a homeless male, approximately thirty years old. Naked, but the filthy hands and hair, jail tattoos, nasty toenails suggested homeless. Two uniforms were standing by, probably the first officers on the scene. One, a patrol cop with a field training officer pin on her uniform. The other, probably her rookie, was a green snot-nosed shiny-badged kid who looked like he was fourteen. They approached the detectives cautiously, as if the two salty old veteran investigators were either suspects or celebrities. The senior officer addressed Ronny and Gill. "We found the body. We didn't touch anything. He's definitely dead. Rats ate some of his eyes and his privates."

Gil nodded. "That is one of the sure signs of death. You allow a rat to gnaw on your gonads, and you might as well be dead."

The young rookie officer wasn't sure how to respond to that piece of street wisdom, so he just gulped. He really wanted to puke, but not in front of the other cops.

Ronny admonished them. "Do not tell anyone what you saw here, not even other officers, sergeants, watch commanders, anyone. If they press you, call me. This comes from the chief."

"Yes sir."

Gil and Ronny dismissed the officers and examined the body. The deceased had a blunt force trauma impact to the forehead. He was naked and it appeared and smelled as if someone had dumped a bucket of bleach over the body.

"Looks like he was dumped here." Gil observed.

"Yep."

"Just like the rest?" Gil asked somewhat rhetorically.

"Yeah, just like the rest," Ronny replied as they began the crime scene investigation.

Gil heard a car come to a screeching halt down the street. "Oh shit."

Ronny looked up from his work and smiled. Patch was on scene. The tall, lean, and muscular Patrol Sergeant approached them the way he approached everyone, like a gunfighter in a showdown. A slight lean, hand comfortably relaxed near his weapon, and hawklike eyes peering into the soul of his opponent. Except these weren't opponents, they were his colleagues, which didn't matter to Patch. Everyone is a threat until they aren't. Then they're still a threat. Paranoia runs deep in the soul of good cops. Patch lived by the code his first watch commander told him long ago when he was a rookie, *I'll trust you just fine when you're dead.*

Gil, always skeptical of Patch's extraordinary luck at scrounging leads for Homicide's toughest cases, marched over and intercepted the veteran patrol sergeant. "This is a closed scene, Patch."

Patch engaged his bullshit generator. "It's okay Gil, the City Manager sent me. Top priority."

Gil shook his head in disbelief. "What?"

"Yeah, special assignment," Patch said with nonchalant confidence.

Gil didn't believe it, but he also knew it was possible. Word on the street was that Patch had a guardian angel watching over him from city hall. Crossing him was risky. "Nobody said anything to me," he groused.

Patch went into condescending mode. "That's why it's special, Gil." Patch got serious and went into sergeant mode. "They just want me to get a look and report on how far the perimeter should expand and determine if we need to close traffic and airspace from news helicopters. You don't think I care about your stupid-ass case, do you? I have ten priority calls holding in the precinct and two guys off sick. A dead bum doesn't come into play, pal. I can't babysit Homicide all day for you pussies."

Gil didn't like it, but he didn't want to risk pissing off the city manager either. Plus, he was a little afraid of Patch. "Fine. Talk to your buddy." He gestured towards Ronny. "I don't give a shit." Gil stomped off back to his car to get his gloves and evidence bags.

Ronny and Patch huddled near the body as Ronny gave a rapid information dump. "This is really the fifth one. Each got a blunt instrument to the front of the head. Then the body is stripped, dumped, and what seems to be a few gallons of bleach poured over. All homeless, no clear victim profile. Two women, three men, ages twenty to fifty, black, Hispanic, white."

"I thought there were only four."

"There might be as many as six. We have a missing person that I think might turn up. To be honest, it might be eight or more. We have some earlier deceased homeless cases we are having the medical examiner take another look at. They might have been earlier practice runs.

"Bottom line?"

"Serial killer, snatches from the city core, murders elsewhere, dumps back here. No motive, no nothing."

"Why the information lockdown?"

"I have no idea. They are releasing the story in trickles, saying that it is health related, like a flu bug the street people have. Seriously, they won't even let us search the VICAP data base for this."

"Why?"

"Again, no clue. It's unprecedented. It's like they're sabotaging us for some reason."

"Shit."

"You better get out of here, Patch. And please, keep *all* this to yourself or it's my ass, brother."

"No problem. I'll give you anything I can find."

"Stay safe."

"Never."

Patch walked out of the scene more puzzled than before he arrived. Why would someone at the top cover up bum murders? What kind of psycho would commit these kinds of kills? A drifter from out of town? People don't just wake up and become a serial killer. Our asshole chief is letting somebody hamstring this investigation. Why?

Patch was pissed off. "Not on my streets, you sons of bitches."

***

Half-a-block down the street, a lone figure in a floppy black hat waited in a car... watching.

Police Headquarters

Chief Hinkley sat behind his desk, locked in his office. He made a phone call to City Hall on his personal cell phone.

"Yeah, chief," the voice answered.

"What am I supposed to do on this serial murder case?"

"If you want to keep your job and your political aspirations, you won't do a damned thing. In fact, maybe Homicide Division is a little fat. Some of those slugs should be moved out to patrol."

"Like I did to Bell?"

"Yeah, like that. You can find a reason. Slow them down."

"What about Father Brannigan? Is this case really why he's here?"

"Who?"

"Brannigan. The Vatican cop. He's everywhere. He has to be on to us." Chief Hinkley wondered, Why is this string-puller at City Hall pretending like they don't know who Father Brannigan is? That's like not knowing who George Washington is. Maybe it's a test.

"Vatican?" the voice asked.

"Yes! And now more of them are coming."

"More what?"

"Pope agents... I don't know what they call them. Secret agents from the Vatican. Brannigan's men. I hear they are all former Swiss Special Forces."

"What? That's crazy talk."

"It's on the news... every friggin' channel is covering it. It has to be true."

"What? Really? Well, we have everything covered. They can't prove anything. Keep me posted."

"Yeah, but..."

The other party disconnected.

"You're going to leave me hanging out to dry. I know it," Hinkley whined out loud.

Mesa Drive and Southern Avenue

Sergeant Harry 'Slay' Bell rolled up to a four-car injury traffic accident his day shift patrol squad was working alongside Traffic Division. Bell's officers were doing traffic control while the motorcycle officers worked the crash investigation.

The motor sergeant on scene, Dave Rose, waved. "Slay, what the hell are you doing out on the street? Did somebody announce a sale on donuts?"

"I'm protecting my city, dipshit. Fighting real crime, not measuring skid marks."

Rose laughed. "Good to see you, Slay."

"You too, brother. How are things?"

Rose turned and scanned his block-long accident scene. "Good. We'll have the street opened up in ten minutes. This is covered. All good."

Slay quickly turned away to listen to a call on the radio, decided it didn't require his attention, then turned his focus back toward the accident scene. "I'm always sad to see a classic like that get taken to the auto graveyard." He pointed at a lime green totaled out AMC Gremlin being towed away.

Rose laughed again, then asked Slay a serious question. "So how are you adjusting to working patrol again after all those years in Homicide?"

"To be honest, it's a nice break. Regular hours, my phone doesn't ring at three in the morning, and very few of my days involve decomposed bodies and autopsies."

Rose chirped like Charlie Sheen, "Winning."

It was Bell's turn to laugh. "I'll be honest, Rose. I wish I could go back. I miss it. How are things in traffic?"

"If I can stay on Motors forever, I will."

Slay said, "I tried to get on Motors, but that damned IQ test..."

"You failed it?" Rose asked.

"No, I passed it."

Both men laughed.

Rose said to him, "You belong in Homicide, Slay. If you were there, all these bum murders would be wrapped by now."

"I think there's more to those cases than meets the eye. I'm better off being out. My ways of case management aren't appreciated by this new style of police management."

Rose didn't believe Sergeant 'Slay' Bell *ever* wanted out of any case. "Yeah, right... Hey, let's get lunch tomorrow."

"Can't. Taking the day off for a doctor's appointment, then the next shift after I get back, I have a ride-along scheduled with a Citizen Review Board member."

Rose made a face of disgust. "That sucks."

"No, not this time. The board member is a retired cop. Do you remember hearing about Lieutenant Frank Bailey?"

"From the 80s? The Special Investigations Unit guy?" Rose asked.

"Yeah, from the ancient times, when men were men and sheep were nervous."

"Back when if you fought a cop, you went to County Hospital instead of jail?"

"When cops carried revolvers that they loaded from bullet loops on their belts like banditos on the border."

"When you could pursue a suspect until the wheels fell off the patrol car or everybody crashed?"

"Yeah, when you could give a troublemaker a nightstick shampoo and never write a report."

"Wow."

"They say Bailey had to kill the chief when he was on the job. He had something wrong with him. Like Old Yeller or something."

"The chief had rabies?"

"I don't really know. Maybe. Some of this stuff is rumors. Those were different times."

Rose paused in thought for a moment. "Wait, is *that*

the guy who shot the mugger in the nuts?"

"Yeah, that's the guy."

"*He's* on the review board?" Rose's eyes widened like an Indiana tourist gazing into the Grand Canyon for the first time.

Bell said to him, "Yeah, it was Mayor Hank's last big middle finger to the city. He got Bailey a permanent seat."

"I heard him and some detective named Quintero got drunk one night and burned down a motorcycle gang's headquarters."

Bell confirmed. "Same guy. Somebody told me that he actually invented the choke hold, but the dates don't seem quite right. That hold has been around for quite a while. History from back then is a little fuzzy. It was before computers."

Rose appeared duly impressed. "Damn… what a week. First Father Brannigan and now Bailey. It's like fate might finally be favoring the thin blue line for a change."

"Father Brannigan? Who's that?" Bell asked.

"Everyone's talking about it, Slay. He's the Vatican Task Force leader, right out of downtown Rome, Italy. They're running a big investigation here. Something called Operation Shining Star. It was on the news," Rose explained. "He's blowing the lid off all the corruption. Something about demons in the jail got it started… or something like that."

"Fuck!" Bell exclaimed as enthusiastically as a college football player finding out he's a first round NFL draft pick.

"Yeah," Rose agreed, excited as that college kid's dad.

Slay attempted to put his feelings into serious words.

"It *is* like fate. Law enforcement is *finally* catching a seriously needed break."

Rose said to Bell, "We're overdue, brother. With all the cop-haters at City Hall, in the media, and in Washington... we needed this."

"We sure did. Definitely overdue," Bell agreed.

"True."

Bell's forehead wrinkled like a scientist examining a new germ warfare specimen under a microscope. "We'll need a code name for Bailey before those assholes at City Hall try to take him down, because they definitely will."

"Definitely."

Bell said, "I'll ask Jones, he usually takes point on stuff like this. He can be trusted. He hates everybody, but he hates everybody equally. But keep it between us for now. You know how crazy shit gets spread around the PD.

Rose affirmed Slay's concern. "Yeah, *we* don't want to be part of any bullshit rumor spreading. It wouldn't be professional."

Slay continued, "And text me right away if you hear any more about the Vatican Task Force. I'm Catholic. I need to know what the fuck is going on." Slay did a few Signs of the Cross just as a precaution.

"Will do," Rose said, trying to mimic the gesture.

Slay looked at Rose's signum crucis attempt quizzically. "I thought you were Mormon?"

"I am. This is just mutual aid. We all got to stick together when jail demons come into play."

Screeching tires and the sound of twisted metal interrupted their conversation. A gawking tourist from Minnesota behind the wheel of an old Buick had slowed down in traffic to stare at the accident scene. Evidently, Minnesota doesn't have traffic accidents, so it was a vacation highlight for him. As the Buick pumped the brakes, an Apache Junction redneck chugging his tenth energy drink of the day, speeding behind him in a Chevy truck that was lifted so high it looked like the frame took an elevator to the fourth floor, rolled a giant tire over Buick's trunk. In seconds after their collision, both drivers were in the street screaming at each other.

Rose shrugged. "I'm surprised it didn't happen sooner."

"Accidents beget more accidents. It's the way of traffic. Back to work, brother."

"Life in the big city, pal."

The two veteran cops knuckle bumped and parted.

CHAPTER 6

Bailey was glad it was winter in Arizona. It was much easier to change one's appearance this time of year. Unfortunately, the Father Brannigan story had gone completely off the rails. The television news lady with the historic cleavage had been doing follow-up stories on the Vatican Task Force operation ever since the Jones ride-along. Fortunately, Possum Momma had never been located and interviewed directly. *God only knows what she would tell them.* The original nexus of the story seemed to be some mix of events, including the firefighters at the scene saving the stabbing victim and Bailey's contrived interaction with Possum Momma. Then, the crowd at the parking lot, responding officers, firefighters, ambulance drivers, a few ride-share drivers, a street preacher, some random local bums, and the tow truck drivers called to haul the arrested parties' vehicles, all seemed to have contributed unique pieces to the legend. It was in the parking lot during the arrests and follow-up investigation where the misinterpreted and imagined information percolated and then evolved into the Father Brannigan story. From there, it took on a life of its own. In fact, one local tow truck driver had been interviewed, claiming to be a witness to the entire incident. A YouTube clip of an alleged 'unedited' version of his interview went viral.

In the clip, the driver, a somewhat cross-eyed man in

his fifties with a week's growth of thick, grizzly beard and a black ball cap bearing a logo that said *Love Machine* in pink letters covering his gray mullet, elaborated for the camera. The tow driver claimed that as he pulled up, the baby was breathing and the mother, a red-headed saintly young girl, was waving goodbye to a man dressed in black with a black hat and cape. The reporter asked the tow truck driver if the man was wearing a priest's garb. The tow truck operator replied, "It looked more like Batman to me, but it could have been a priest, if Batman was a Catholic. But I don't know what religion Batman is. I always thought he was probably an Episcopalian." Then the driver pulled a small metal flask out of his pocket and offered the reporter a sip of the contents before the cameraman cut the feed.

Bailey watched the video at least twenty times before he decided it was probably safe to go back out in public. Nobody *really* knows what Father Brannigan looks like… probably.

Nevertheless, he had developed a subtle disguise since he wrote the list, adding a few things to change his appearance in the remote event that Possum Momma, Possum Baby, or the knocked-out boyfriend ever spotted him again. *Possum Baby likely won't talk for at least another three years, so I got that going for me.*

Bailey took a few days to grow out his whiskers and then had a local barber tint his hair and stubble to a very faint brown, giving him a more youthful appearance. *I could easily pass for sixty.* He found his nice raincoat and had it dry cleaned. He dug his dress hat out of storage and brushed it. It seemed to Bailey like wearing a shirt and tie from now on, rather than a polo, was in order. Finally, he added some slightly yellow-tinted, wire-frame glasses to his look, also ordering a pair in his prescription. *It feels good to change up my style a bit.*

From his undercover experience years before, he knew modifying just a few things could significantly reduce the possibility of being recognized, even by someone who knows you well, at least at first glance. Bailey felt like he was ready to go out in the world again. The Phoenix winter this time of year made the coat, hat, and necktie feel appropriate and comfortable. *Yes, I'm ready*, he thought. *Not even Possum Mama can stop me now.* It was time to schedule the next ride-along.

He punched the number into his phone for Ma Donna, the veteran burglary detective.

"Detective Kennedy."

"Detective, this is Frank Bailey. I'm a member of the Citizen Review Board. I was hoping to schedule some time to work with you."

"*The* Frank Bailey," she asked?

"Well, I suppose so. I'm not aware of another one."

Ma Donna said bluntly, "I heard you killed the chief when you were a cop, lieutenant."

Man, kill one chief and you're a chief killer for life. "No, not at all. We argued, then later that day, he had a heart attack. Totally unrelated incidents."

"*Right.*"

"Seriously."

"Sure, whatever you say. Statute of limitations. I totally get it, sir."

Bailey felt a sense of frustration welling up. "Well, I most certainly did NOT kill the Chief, detective. So, please do *not* spread that rumor around."

"Didn't kill him. Got it. *Right*."

I give up. "Can you please focus on my question. Might we schedule a ride-along?"

"I'd love to, sir. I'm heading out in an hour to do interviews. Can I pick you up on the way?"

"Yes. Perfect. Thank you, Detective. If it means anything, you were highly recommended by Mayor Henry. He was my old partner."

The mention of Mayor Henry made Ma Donna even more chatty. "That's *so* kind of him. We all loved Mayor Henry. I hated to see him retire. He was a great police chief too. Our new chief is a dick, excuse my French. You know, sir, I already feel like I can trust you. After all, since you had to kill a dickhead chief when you were on the job, you'd understand better than anyone. I have to tell you, sir, that story is still effen legend around here. Respect! Give me your address. I'll text you when I'm out front."

Bailey, gave up on defending his innocence of the crime of murder, recited his address, then went about preparing for another adventure on the street. *But this time, no Father Brannigan shenanigans.*

Mesa PD Criminal Investigations - Burglary Unit

Detective Donna 'Ma Donna' Fitzgerald Kennedy didn't trust many people, but everyone in the detective division seemed to trust her. She was like the division mom. Ma Donna was an ancient fixture in CID, working burglary cases for over a decade. After the call from Bailey, she gathered her squad-mates and updated them on her latest gem of gossip. Circled by Don 'Stinky' Carter, Ellen 'Belle' Starr, Terry 'Fats' Growzinski, and Fredrick 'Gay Freddy' Wilson, she shared her breaking news.

"Guess who's riding around with me today, losers?"

she said with typical detective sarcasm, cynicism, and faux disdain for her co-workers.

Cynical detectives make cynical deductions. One by one, they threw out their guesses. "The Governor? Neil Armstrong? Durwood Kirby? Oprah?"

"Who the hell is Durwood Kirby?" Stinky Carter asked.

Fats Growzinki appeared offended. "Greatest television entertainer of all time. He sold Timex watches."

Gay Freddy disagreed. "That was John Cameron Swayze, moron."

Belle Starr piped in, "Can I change my guess to Brad Pitt?"

Ma Donna was pissed. *These turds are worse than my four kids.* "Shut up, assholes. I'll have retired Lieutenant Frank Bailey riding with me today. The old SIU guy from the eighties who is on the Citizen Review Board now."

Gay Freddy perked up. "Is he the one that killed that shit bag chief back in the day?"

"Yes! He strangled him right at his desk, and the Homicide detectives covered it up. That kind of thing was fairly normal back then. At least that's what people say," Ma Donna declared.

Freddy stiffened, "No shit?"

"I'm fairly confident that's how it went down. A few years ago, a drunk pawn shop detail detective at a choir practice in Falcon Park let it slip that he heard it from a retired deputy chief who made him swear not to repeat it. It doesn't get more reliable than that."

Fats added, "I heard Bailey shot some piece of shit in the nuts for beating up an old lady."

Belle said, "Good. That's how cops used to handle things. We need to bring that shit back."

"Hell yeah! Damn right! Overdue!" the group replied with enthusiasm.

Assuming high-fives were still a thing, Ma Donna awkwardly attempted to give everyone a high-five for their team spirit. "I'll give you guys a full report when I get back. It should be an interesting day. We needed a guy like Bailey for years. This is the hero we have been waiting for."

She headed to her cubicle to gather her equipment and hit the street.

Gay Freddy asked, "Isn't he about a hundred years old now? Just ewww. What's a smelly old fossil going to do?"

Fats gave him a slight warning shove. "In the Bible, Zeus was like a million years old, and he could still kick ass, you disrespectful little worm."

Stinky gave Fats a shove. "That was Methuselah, you heathen idiot. Read the Bible!"

Belle shoved Stinky, "Leave them alone, butthole. The only book I ever saw you reading was a stupid ass Bronco Hammer book."

"Hey, I read the Bible!"

"When?" Belle challenged.

"I mean, I mostly skimmed some of it, but I got the gist enough to know Zeus wasn't in it."

Fats jumped back in with another shove, "You don't know that for sure, idiot. I was talking about that other Zeus ... from uh, Egypt."

Soon, everyone was shoving as the biblical history debate became more heated.

Ma Donna gave a shrill whistle and went into squad den mother mode. "Knock it off, maggots! Don't make me come back here and beat your sorry asses. Now go write your reports and behave. This is why we can't have nice things!"

The foursome broke it up and began wandering back to their own cubicles in shame after being scolded by Ma.

Stinky made a pitiful attempt at an excuse. "Sorry, Ma. But Freddy started it."

The rest of the squad fired stares of betrayal at him as Ma angrily pointed a finger. He hung his head and shuffled away in disgrace and shame.

"Nobody likes a rat, Stinky," Ma declared, knowing he was probably telling the truth.

I should ground every one of those rowdy sons of bitches, she thought as she loaded her briefcase, purse, and tactical bag over her weary 'Ma' shoulders and shuffled off to the elevator.

Bailey's Apartment

Bailey saw a text message from a new number: *LT - Det Kennedy - out front.* He put the phone in his pocket, grabbed his hat and coat, then headed for the street.

Out front, he saw a Ford Focus with a stout, Irish female cop at the wheel who looked to be in her mid-to-late thirties. *I didn't know Ford put out a car color called misery gray. That's one depressing-looking car.*

The occupant waved. He hopped in and offered his hand. Ma Donna shook it and immediately took control of the conversation. "You don't have to say a thing, Lieutenant. We all know who you are."

Shit! They know I'm Father Brannigan!

Ma Donna continued, "We know you're the one who is going to save the city. We've been waiting for someone *old school* to make things right for a long time, sir."

Bailey concealed his relief. *At least they don't think I'm the man from the Vatican.* "I'll do what I can, Detective. But please, just call me Bailey."

"Call me Ma or Donna, unless there are citizens around. Then we have to say Detective and Lieutenant, or they get confused. Citizens don't understand nuance, sir."

"Got it."

"First stop will be at a local burglar's home. I need him to give up a fence. Somebody has been offing merch from residential burgs. I think they are taking it by truck out of state to sell, maybe in yard sales or swap meets."

"Offing merch... fence... burg... I haven't heard those terms for a while." Bailey smiled at hearing the classical words of his people spoken once more.

"I'm trying to speak your language, Mister Bailey. From back in the day."

"Just Bailey."

"Right, I would usually say *the organized receiving and distribution of stolen goods*, but if we are going to save the city, we need to start using the proper vernacular for *real* crime fighting. Like you guys did."

"Right. I suppose so." Bailey agreed, but he wasn't sure why.

Ma parked down the street from a house in a run-down neighborhood. The once middle-class three-bedroom block starter-houses with single carports and cheap wood fences around the backyards, were now poorly maintained low-income rentals. She pointed out one with a broken-down fence without a gate, revealing a camper parked in the backyard.

"He's in there."

"What's his name?"

"William Gordon. But he goes by Sky Hump."

"Interesting choice for a nom de guerre."

"We don't have to worry about him curing cancer, sir."

"Have any leverage?"

"I can arrest him on probable cause for a felony shoplift. He's a suspect in a few business burglaries as part of a local 459 crew. If he flips, he's the small fish we can throw back and still live with ourselves."

Bailey was impressed with her investigative acumen. "What's he look like?"

"White male, twenty-two years old, black hair in a man-bun, tall, skinny, black fingernail polish. He always wears a black tank top and black jeans."

"Got it."

"Oh, and I almost left out. He's an ignorant-looking bastard."

"I'm shocked. How do we get him out?"

"That trailer doesn't have air conditioning. We'll knock first, then I'll spray some air freshener in the window if that doesn't work."

Ma stepped out of the car, drew her full-size duty automatic, slung her massive purse over her shoulder, and marched up to the door.

Bailey followed a few steps behind Ma.

She banged on the side of the trailer, tactically standing off to the side of the entrance and away from the window. "Mesa Police!"

A voice came from inside. "Go away."

"William, dear. It's Ma Kennedy. Come on out here, sweetie. I want you to meet someone."

"Fuck you, Ma."

Ma's backbone stiffened. "Don't sass me, you dirty little shit!"

Sky Hump pressed. "I said go away! I have rights, Ma! Get bent!"

Ma looked at Bailey. "I apologize for this rude little fucker, sir. He didn't have a proper upbringing. Looks like room freshener it is."

"Room freshener?" Bailey asked, wondering what she meant by that.

Ma smiled and dug into her huge purse.

Bailey saw what was coming and quickly stepped back to the street.

Ma pulled out a commercial bear spray container and put the nozzle to the open window. She pulled the pin, pressed the trigger, and gave the trailer a very long version of the recommended three-second blast.

"One Mississippi, the thirty-second largest state by area. Two Mississippi, also called the Magnolia State. Three Mississippi, with Jackson as the capital and largest city."

A few seconds later, a coughing and gagging William 'Sky Hump' Gordon came staggering out the door. Snot was running out of his nose and tears poured out of his eyes like a water faucet. Ma grabbed him by the man-bun, spun him around, and cuffed him behind his back. Then she jerked him across the yard to the sidewalk, away from the growing mushroom cloud of bear spray, and pushed him face down onto the ground.

Bailey, appreciating her style, stayed out of the way and let the veteran detective work. *Some things never change. Excellent police work, Ma.*

Ma began questioning her suspect. "I need a name and an address, shitbird. Who is buying all the shit that you stupid assholes steal?"

Sky Hump wasn't feeling cooperative. "I don't know what you're talking about, Ma. Leave me alone."

Ma used her foot to roll him onto his back. She pointed her gun at his nose. "I'm feeling threatened here, turd. I could have you deported."

Sky Hump remained defiant. "You can't do that, Ma. I was born in Iowa."

"Bullshit. What's the third largest city per capita in Iowa?"

Sky Hump whined. "How the hell would I know that?"

"It's Des Moines, maggot! County Seat of Polk County."

Sky Hump moaned in misery. "I knew that. I just forgot."

Bailey whispered, "You know a lot about geography, Ma.

She whispered back with a polite smile. "I have a degree in education. I'm going to work in the public school system and teach ungrateful little pieces of shit all this crap after I retire."

"Noble."

She turned her attention back to Sky Hump. "You didn't forget. I don't think you've ever even been to Iowa. I ought to revoke your birth certificate right now, you slimy lying worm."

Sky Hump relented and went limp in defeat. He confessed, "Okay, fine, Ma. I'm not here legally. I was born in Toronto and never filed any papers. Dammit, you got me. Please don't kick me out. I have a warrant in Canada."

Ma turned, looked at Bailey, and mouthed, "Who knew? I was just jerking his chain."

Bailey suppressed the urge to smirk.

Ma continued working Sky Hump for information. "So, you *are* a goddamned terrorist!"

Sky Hump squirmed. "Wait, what? No! I said I'm Canadian, Ma. We play hockey!"

Ma yelled in his face, "Foreign terrorist!"

Sky Hump continued whining. "Stop saying that! I didn't do anything. This is bullshit, Ma."

Bailey noticed something. "Ma, do you mind if I ask this guy a couple questions?"

"Sure. We have a few minutes before the bus shows up to take him to Gitmo for terrorism." She winked.

Sky Hump shrieked, "WHAT? Come on, Ma, I'm not a terrorist. I'm an asshole. You know me."

"I thought you said you were Canadian? she yelled.

"I can be both!" Sky Hump argued, feeling like he was making a point, but also feeling like he wasn't saying it right.

Bailey knelt to get a better look at the necklace their suspect was wearing. There was a St. Christopher pendant on it. "Are you Catholic, Mister Gordon?"

"Call me Sky Hump... and yes. Why?"

"Have you heard Father Brannigan is in town?"

Sky Hump suddenly quit being argumentative and became serious. "The demon hunter who saved the baby? Yeah, everybody on the street is talking about it."

"He's not taking any prisoners, Dry Hump."

"Sky Hump!"

"Whatever. He's secretly working with a select few cops, like me and Ma. Don't make her turn your evil ass over to the Vatican police. They can legally burn your ass at the stake, or worse. You'll wish you were in Gitmo. Big mistake. Ever hear of Joan of Arc?

"No, what was she convicted of?"

"Nothing! And they burned her alive anyway. Pope law."

"Shit!"

"We're talking the Holy Roman Empire on your ass, bud."

"Fuck!"

Bailey knew he had him. "Exactly. Now tell Ma everything she wants to know, or I make a phone call to Rome, pal."

Sky Hump folded. "Fine. I'll tell her. But no call to Rome and no Gitmo. Deal?"

"Only if you give her everything you know and then leave town forever."

"Deal." Sky Hump looked at Ma pleadingly. "I'll tell you everything, Ma. Also, I know about a robbery at a liquor store from last week. I just remembered it. I'll give you that too. Please, just let me leave town alive. No Vatican, and no Canada, and no Gitmo. Please, Ma. I'll behave. I mean it. I have an aunt in Fresno I can go live with."

Ma smiled. "Fresno is a good place for you, Sky Hump. I

think you'll fit right in there. It's an environment a young man like you can thrive in." She pinched his cheek, then wiped her hand off on his shirt.

"Thanks, Ma. You were always my favorite Mesa cop."

"You were always in my top one hundred favorite assholes, Sky Hump," Ma Donna said in a very Ma voice.

"Thanks, Ma. That means a lot to me."

Bailey interrupted their mutual admiration society meeting and asked Sky Hump one more thing. "What do you know about bums getting murdered?"

Sky Hump said in a whisper, "I know it ain't the street behind the killings. Those aren't murders, they're assassinations."

"What?" Bailey asked, a bit confused as Sky Hump delivered unexpected information on the case.

"Word is, those murders are a message. And it ain't just murders. People get threatened. Get the shit beat out of them."

"Message?"

"Yeah, a serious message. Get out of town ... Sell all your shit and leave. That's what everyone says. I don't know. I don't have any shit to sell. Except for ... you know, the shit I sell, which I will never do again. So, none of that shit affects me. But that's what I heard. Honest truth."

Ma and Bailey looked at each other. Ma, with increased respect for the old man riding with her. And Bailey, with a bit of fear in his eyes for the can of worms he might have just opened.

City Hall

In the darkness of a stairwell, two persons conferred, one tall, one short.

"These Vatican cops must know."

"I don't think there are really any Vatican cops here. It must be bullshit."

The voice was nervous. "When we made a move to tear down their church for the development project, we went too far. I knew this would happen."

The response was firm but clearly losing patience. "No. You didn't. And nothing happened. It's all rumors. As soon as the last deed clears escrow, we start inflating the prices with the announcement so we can justify rezoning, just like we planned."

"It's been too extreme. We went too far. I want out. We have to stop."

"I'll tell you when to stop. Just keep your mouth shut and get back to work."

The pair exited the stairwell and returned to Council Chambers.

In the shadows, another figure moved, finding an exit and disappearing into the night.

CHAPTER 7

Bailey's Apartment

The shift with Ma Donna had been enlightening, but exhausting. Bailey was fatigued, feeling the years, yet his mind was still diligently working on the puzzle. *What message was Sky Hump talking about?* He hung his coat on the antique wooden hall tree near the front door and went to the kitchen. *It doesn't make sense. Or does it?*

Bailey poured four fingers of Jack Daniel's into a heavy crystal cocktail glass and walked out to his balcony to think. *What would the murder of homeless people accomplish?*

Bailey slipped off his shoes, undid his tie and took a sip of whiskey. The soft burn of whiskey on his throat was calming physically and mentally.

If you want to solve a crime, figure out who benefits from the outcome. This might be what it looks like, just a series of murders, but was it a serial killer or something else? Was there a perverse homicidal degenerate doing this, or someone creating a scenario for the police that would lead them to believe a homicidal degenerate was on the loose?

The evening air was too chilly to sit outside for long. Bailey decided to send an email and go to bed: *Sergeant Bell. If our ride-along is still on schedule, please meet me as planned at ten tomorrow morning. Thank you, Frank Bailey -*

Citizen Review Board.

***

The next morning, Bailey walked to the Castaway coffee shop for his scheduled meeting with Sergeant Harry *Slay* Bell. He had just arrived when a supervisor patrol car rolled up to the curb out front on McDonald. A husky uniform sergeant with blondish hair and an old school cop mustache stepped out and greeted him on the sidewalk out front. His weathered face gave away he was on the backside of his service, perhaps around fifteen years on.

Slay said, "Lieutenant. Nice to finally meet you. I've heard so much about your career."

Bailey was afraid to think what that meant. "Thanks, Sergeant. I've heard great things about you. Mayor Henry, my old partner, thinks quite highly of you."

Slay said to him, "That's nice to hear, sir. Do you want to have a cup of coffee before we hit the street?"

Bailey replied, "That sounds like an excellent idea."

They ordered and sat down together on the outside patio area. They were alone in the small fenced and shaded area, so they could speak freely.

Bell said, "Lieutenant, the department needs new direction from the top, in a big way. I'm glad you're here."

"I'm not sure what I'll be able to do, but if I can make it any better, I promise you I'll give it my best shot."

"That's all anyone can ask. Have you met any other officers?"

"Jones J. Jones and I worked a shift. I like him. He's a good cop."

"Definitely. He's one of the best. He's not what I would

call warm and fuzzy, but if there is a fight, he's the guy you want as a backup."

"And I pulled a shift with a detective they call Ma Donna. Also a great cop."

"Absolutely. It sounds like you've been working with the all-star team so far."

"That's why I'm here. You need to be part of that team. You worked Homicide, right?"

"Right. Many years, sir."

"Please, call me Bailey."

"Let's split the difference and I'll call you lieutenant. You can call me Slay, or if the public is present, Sergeant is fine."

"Perfect. I like that, Slay. Now, about Homicide. Do you know much about the dead homeless person cases?"

"Not much. Someone has that one locked down tight. I'd like to catch the initial call on one though and take a first-hand look. There has to be something at these scenes we can use. I just feel like it might be getting overlooked."

"Why do you say that?"

"They compartmentalize every unit, forensics, homicide, patrol. Nobody is allowed to talk to anybody. No sharing of information. It's bullshit."

"Why?"

"Nobody knows… it comes from above, like City Hall level above. At least that's what I hear around the campfire."

"No shit?"

"Yeah. It's bad."

Interesting."

"Very interesting. I feel like there is something going on." Slay took a sip of coffee and continued. "It's something big. We're just talking intuition here, but I don't think this is your typical serial killer or standard degenerate psychopath. This is a special kind of psychopath. The worst kind."

"What kind is that, Slay?"

"The successful kind. The kind no one knows is a psychopath until it's too late. The kind who works their way to the top of the food chain. And this one is working a huge scam. I don't think these killings are for prurient interests. It isn't a sexual or old-school horror movie degenerate. I think we have a traditional criminal motive behind the killings, making them look like a pervert or psycho. We just can't see it yet."

"Wow."

"Yeah, if we had shared briefings and a murder board, we could get these ideas out there and brainstorm them. But it isn't going to happen. Not with this regime. If I didn't know better, I'd almost think the investigation was being undermined."

"Sad."

Bailey finished his last sip of coffee and changed the subject. "Why don't you show me what a day shift patrol sergeant does."

Slay grinned. "Cool. Let's have fun."

The first squawk on the radio was an alarm at a bank.

"Usually bullshit." Slay explained. "But we have to follow protocol. A new manager probably forgot the alarm code."

"Some things never change."

The bank robbery alarm procedure was textbook. The squad was all experienced officers. An officer typically didn't get day shift without seniority.

Everyone moved into position with invisible deployment, quietly taking wide perimeter positions surrounding the bank, and waiting for dispatch to receive the routine *all clear* notification from a bank manager.

"Oh well, shit!" Slay muttered as they rolled up.

A dark blue SUV was parked in the street. The man behind the wheel was wearing a ski mask.

Bailey smiled. "So, you get these false alarms a lot?" He pointed at the SUV. "That guy must be the new manager who forgot the alarm code."

Slay gave him an evil grin. "Yeah. Well... not this time. We got a live one." Slay began directing units.

Bailey subconsciously checked his weapon. He had a bad feeling.

Slay said to him, "Do you mind waiting in the car, Lieutenant? I need to go fix this real quick."

"Not at all. Not my clowns, not my circus."

"Thanks."

Slay stepped out of the car, retrieved a twelve-gauge shotgun out of the trunk, verified he had a rifled slug in the chamber, then moved up to a position of cover behind the concrete pillar of a walkway shade.

Three more men in ski masks came out of the bank across the street from him.

Slay stepped out and recited verbatim the professional warning he learned from his academy training. Or perhaps he paraphrased it. "Freeze, assholes. Mesa Police."

The driver fired a round from behind the wheel. It

went wild.

Slay fired a rifled slug into the front left tire of the suspect vehicle, then jacked a shell of double aught buck into the chamber and shot the driver.

Watching, Bailey's heart raced like an old thoroughbred tied up beside the racetrack when the starter pistol fires. *I would have popped the driver first.*

Another officer took a position to Slay's right. Slay gave her the shotgun, drew his duty weapon and ran at the low ready towards the men who were now on the other side of the SUV.

An officer down the street from the front of the SUV gave cover, emptying a magazine at the robbers and driving them to the rear of their vehicle where Slay exchanged fire with them.

Diving and rolling as nimbly as a middle-aged overweight cop in a bullet proof vest can dive and roll, Slay came up in a kneeling position and mag-dumped the trio, putting them all down.

The rest of the officers moved in and secured the scene.

Bailey left the car, lit a cigarette, and walked up to a now standing, but clearly exhausted, Slay. "I sure hope those assholes weren't undercover janitors."

Slay chuckled. "Yeah, me too. Sorry to cut your ride-along short, Lieutenant. It looks like I'll be tied up all day with this."

"No problem. it was nice to see you in action, Slay. You lived up to how Mayor Henry described you. I can walk home from here. It's only a few blocks."

"Sounds good, sir."

"And let's talk again soon about the bum murders. I have some ideas," Bailey suggested.

"I'd like that, sir. Me too. I'll keep in touch."

The men shook hands.

Bailey walked home.

It was a good day.

Police Headquarters - Burglary Unit

Ma Donna held court with her squad, all anxious to hear about her adventures with the new Review Board member.

The squad blasted her with questions as she sat behind her desk. "What was he like? Was he super old? Did he need a mobility scooter? Do you think he wears an adult diaper?" The questions flew from every angle.

Ma put a hand up and settled them down. "First, he wasn't that old. Well, he *was* old, but super spry. No, not spry, but he seemed like a regular detective, but older. Not geezer old... but he looked like a typical retired cop."

Gay Freddy asked, "You mean fat and drunk in a Hawaiian shirt and cargo shorts?"

"No, not at all, in fact he was dressed kind of weird, like a British spy or some old 1940s detective out of a black and white TV show."

Freddy wasn't impressed. "That's so gay."

"No, he isn't gay, he looked like an old school guy on a mission. He had on a fedora and a dark trench coat, silk necktie... he looked pretty nice really. Just different than you usually see around here."

Gay Freddy changed his mind. "Oh, I take it all back. Totally Hetero. I simply adore him."

'Fats' Growzinski said, "Wait a minute, what kind of mission? I thought he was here to save the police department. Isn't that his mission? Why do you need a hat and tie for *that*? He probably should have a turtleneck and army pants like that movie guy who does those improbable missions. He's old now too."

Detective 'Belle' Starr wasn't having it. "Oh, blow it out your keister, Fats. Just because a man wants to look nice doesn't mean he can't have *two* missions. And your movie guy did like nine missions. What the hell is wrong with you. That's pretty racist."

Fats appeared confused.

'Stinky' Carter agreed with Belle. "Yeah, he definitely sounds like he's capable of two missions. Hell, I think I could do at least three missions."

Fats replied, "You left a mission in the men's room this morning that was impossible. What the hell did you eat last night, Stinky?"

Stinky groused. "I got a condition. Fuck you!"

The shoving started again, but Ma intervened before it got out of control this time and softly slapped each combatant once with a quick *shut the fuck up,* loud enough to get their attention but quiet enough not to be noticed by the other squads stationed on the second floor. Then she addressed the group again. "Now, if you rude douche bags will knock it off for a minute, there's more to this. If you'd shut your filthy pie holes, I could finish telling you."

The reply was a chorus of *sorry ma's.*

She began again. "So, Bailey and I delivered some old-time religion to Sky Hump and he started spouting off. He spilled his guts. We really put the squeeze on that turd."

"Why are you talking like that?" Stinky asked.

"Because if our department is going to get saved, we better all start talking like real cops again instead of community-college philosophy students, you pussy. And we better start kicking some ass on the street again. Bailey can't do this by himself."

The other three detectives looked at Stinky Carter like he just farted in an air lock.

Belle added, "Lieutenant Bailey *and* Father Brannigan."

"Of course. I think that goes without saying," Ma agreed.

Freddy and Fats did a quick sign of the cross just in case Father Brannigan was watching.

Ma continued. "But here's where it gets interesting. Bailey takes a run at this maggot and goes straight to Catholicism. He spots the St. Christopher medal on Sky Hump and starts asking about the bum murders."

The detectives fell into a state of awe. It was a plot twist in the criminal investigations division the likes of which none of them had never experienced before. The lowly burglary detectives suddenly thrust into the heart of a serial murder case. Things really *were* changing!

Ma elaborated. "So, *then* Bailey finds out all these bum murders have something to do with crime, not perverts. Somebody is sending a *message*. And..." She dramatically paused, "later he told me there might be a property crime involved." Ma wasn't exactly sure if that was what Bailey said or if it was what she wished he said, but she was in the moment.

Belle squealed. "Ewwwww."

Ma asked, "What's the matter?"

"Stinky's got a boner."

Freddy squealed, "Ewwwww."

Stinky Carter tried to wiggle it away, "I got a condition. This is totally case related. I'm protected by HIPPA. There is a prescription in my desk."

Ma reached over and flicked the projection in front of Stinky's pants hard with a snap of her finger. The boner instantly disappeared. "Keep that thing out of my face, Carter, or I'll kick your ass, condition or not."

Fats asked, shocked at witnessing a medical miracle. "Where did you learn that, Ma?"

"I was a Candy Striper in the hospital when I was a kid. A night shift nurse taught me. It's a technique you have to master. It comes in handy if you have pre-teen boys in the house. They're disgusting little bastards. Like Stinky."

Stinky decided to repent. "Sorry everybody. I just got caught up in the moment."

Ma replied. "Forget it. It happens. I mean, in all fairness, that was some monumental news. I was a little aroused myself when I heard about it to be honest."

The squad mates hung their heads in a subtle admission to being all a bit excited as well.

Ma continued. "Now, back to Bailey. We think there is a lot more detail to this deal. It appears someone killed these people for a reason, maybe trying to make it look like a serial killer. But that ain't all."

"What else," Fats asked.

"I think Bailey might be working with Father Brannigan. I don't have any proof of that, but he knew a lot about Brannigan's operation. They're already taking prisoners. I think they're going medieval on 'em."

"What?"

"Yeah, these Vatican Task Force guys can disappear assholes and ship them to the Vatican for torture and questioning. It's Italian Gitmo for any local shit stains who pissed off the Pope."

Belle asked, "Is Bailey Italian?"

Ma said, "No, he looks like he's from Scottsdale."

Gay Freddy said, "He sounds scrumptious. I just want to put him in my pocket and think about him all day."

Fats gave Freddy a dirty look, "What the hell does that mean?"

"It means I like him. That's all. He's going to save the PD. He's the hero we've all been waiting for. Between him and Father Brannigan we finally have a fighting chance. And for once, we lowly property crime dicks might, just maybe, get a shot at breaking a serial killer case. It will be the burglary unit's finest hour."

Stinky smiled at the thought of the burglary unit's finest hour, then appeared uncomfortable and dashed back to his cubicle, walking oddly half-bent over.

Ma admonished the remaining squad members, "Keep this between us. Nobody can know about this case. I'm going to try to find out if anyone else is working with Bailey and Brannigan so we can coordinate with them. Now get back to work. We have a Police Department to save. And start talking and acting like real cops," she gave each one of them an official Ma stink-eye, "you bunch of pussies."

The detectives grinned ornery grins, showing their teeth like old dogs snarfing down treats.

Heavenly Saint Catholic Church - Rectory

Father Garcia went through the books one more time. Feeding the needy was his life's work. But the population he attended to had dropped to just a few dozen, right after having two years of record numbers. And now, the city was talking about an eminent domain offer to tear down the church and move his flock to a new building near the industrial area by the freeway.

Garcia wasn't on board. Something was wrong. He couldn't quite put his finger on it. The whole thing felt as though it had been created by design, the surge, the drop off, the offer.

Being the priest of a downtown church in a declining city core was challenging. Some of his parishioners were Mexican nationals, or at least they had been. Many were the local homeless. The homeless were reliable parishioners, and now they were gone. The older residents who attended were dying off and the area was being rapidly being taken over by developers, who were bulldozing aging residences and rezoning land to commercial. There was more large swaths of vacant land than houses or businesses now.

Maybe I should take the offer. There is little hope for my little church here.

The elderly priest prayed.

Bailey's Apartment

Frank hadn't witnessed bad guys getting lit up for a long time. His heart was still racing. He might have acted nonchalant at the scene, but that was just his training and experience. The leader can never get rattled or show stress in front of the troops, even when he's not the leader anymore. But afterwards, when you get home and you're alone, you drop the guardrails and cope the best you can.

It was only a little before lunchtime, but Bailey poured a drink. *Alcohol is cheaper and faster than therapy.*

Bailey snatched a notepad off the kitchen counter and started scribbling down some ideas. Slay felt there was more going on with the murders. *I trust Slay's instincts. More going on.* Sky Turd or whatever his name was thought it was planned assassinations intended to send a message. *Planned as a warning. But to who and why?* The whole force was locked out of the case. *How do I get inside the team working these murders?*

Bailey took one sip of his cocktail, then he rethought his purpose. He put the glass back in the refrigerator for later. *I need to keep my wits about me.* He made a pot of coffee and made a phone call. *If someone is willing to stack bum bodies downtown for nefarious purposes, they won't hesitate to whack a geezer cop who asks too many questions. A geezer like me. I need professional muscle.*

Bailey made a call.

Jones J. Jones picked up on the first ring. "Jones."

"It's Frank Bailey."

"No, it isn't. It's Blue Moses. You need to get in the habit of using code names, sir."

"Well, what's your code name?"

"Buffalo Soldier."

Cool. "Right. Let me start over. It's Blue Moses."

"What do you need, sir?"

"I'm making a move on the bum murders. I'll need a backup."

"I have three days off coming and I've never used a vacation day or sick day, so I'll be free as long as you need me. I'll pack a bag and be at your place in an hour. You have a spare room, right?"

Bailey wasn't prepared for that level of enthusiasm. "Yeah, uh, I have an office with a fold-out couch in it that's pretty nice. But you don't have to do that, Jones. I just need some cover for when I'm working this thing."

"I'll be there in an hour. I have more to report but not on the phone."

Jones disconnected.

"Shit, now what have I done?" Bailey asked himself.

He went to the office to prepare for his new welcome, but uninvited, roommate. *I guess Buffalo Soldier lives here now. I better get a few hundred pounds of raw meat and fifty gallons of beer delivered.*

Police Headquarters — Chief's Office

Chief Hinkley had his executive team seated around him in the spacious conference room. He delivered his news as confidently as he could, knowing there would be significant pushback, even from the sycophants.

The dark paneling of the room set the mood. There was seldom good news discussed here. The thick brown carpet deadened the sound of the voices and interfered with the movement of everyone's chairs. The photos of previous chiefs adorning the walls looked down in seeming disgust at the group, or at least one of the executive staff thought so.

Chief Hinkley began, "We're getting nowhere with the homeless homicides investigations, so, I am going to shake things up." He made an odd gesture as if shaking a baby to reinforce his intent. Everyone squirmed uncomfortably in their seats in reaction to the bizarre display. He continued, impervious to their discomfort.

"I'm pulling two detectives out of Homicide Division and transferring them to Central Division Patrol. Having more beat cops will certainly be more helpful than more detectives just shuffling paper. The investigation so far has led nowhere with the current staffing. So, I'd like to have Detective Ronny Cortez and Detective Thomas Beechum moved to Patrol division by end of business today. We'll make a press announcement about it. The public information officer will explain how we are changing up the game in response to the latest findings."

Deputy Chief Bill Spooner leaned back in his chair and asked, "What findings? So far, we don't know anything. I've never seen one report coming out of the Criminal Investigations Division on this. Why is that?"

"Investigative purposes, Spooner," the Chief groused. "You attended the FBI academy. I thought you would know that."

"I know that when there isn't any communication, nothing happens on a case. This should be an all-hands-on deck operation."

The Chief pointed a finger and scolded him. "That's enough, Bill. I don't need your chronic negativity."

Spooner simply smiled and folded his hands in front of him. He wouldn't be baited by the Chief's bullshit childish tactics. There *was* more going on here. He'd find out *what* it was one way or the other. *Hinkley is an out-of-town political hack and there is no way I'm letting him destroy Mesa PD.*

Bailey's Apartment

Jones J. Jones arrived with a large canvas bag and a long plastic case that Bailey suspected was probably full of weapons. He was dressed in jeans, a black T-shirt,

SWAT boots, and a black Kangol cap worn backwards.

"Come in and get comfortable, Jones."

"Buffalo soldier, sir."

"In the apartment let's just go with last names. Jones and Bailey. If anyone shows up, we can switch into code names. Will that work?"

"Sure. Just being cautious, sir."

"Bailey."

"Right.

Bailey showed him where to stow his gear, where his bathroom was, and where the food was. As soon as he was settled, they sat together on the balcony with coffees.

Jones said. "I'll need your schedule."

"I don't have a schedule. My day is fairly random, Jones."

Jones warned, "You don't make a move outside the apartment without me, sir."

"Well, I was going to try to schedule a ride-along tonight with Detective Edgewater Patterson. But I should be fine."

"Gumby?"

"Yeah."

"They say he can see the future."

"No shit?"

"That's what they say. If he makes a prediction, you better believe it."

"I'll try to remember that."

"I'll follow you from a block back. Tell Gumby I'm there."

"Do you think that's necessary?"

"There's blood in the water, sir. There are people who don't want you here. Especially with Father Brannigan in town. We're on the verge of greatness. They will stop at nothing to take either of you out."

Bailey was dubious but didn't want to argue with Jones.

"If you are going to follow to protect me, then take my car. It's the least I can do."

"Thanks. Good idea."

Bailey gave Jones the keys and then went to his room to call and see if he could schedule the ride-along. He looked over his shoulder before closing his door to see Jones knocking out some fingertip pushups while he waited.

CHAPTER 8

Detective Edgewater Patterson, AKA Gumby, sat in his undercover fleet black 1985 Buick Grand National and pondered his future. The brass had been trying to pull him out of the Special Investigations Unit for the last six months. They were trying to remove all the senior detectives from specialty units. His Special Investigations Unit chain of command had successfully helped him avoid transfer with a series of *delay, distract, and mislead* style tactics. So far, he had avoided drawing attention to himself and getting on the executive team's radar. Then his phone rang.

"Detective Patterson, this is Frank Bailey from the Citizen's Review Board."

"Yes."

"I was hoping to schedule a ride-along with you tonight."

"Why?"

"Well, it's sort of what I do."

"I can't see how we can possibly arrange it, for your own safety. I will need to terminate this call for security purposes. We are working a Homeland Security related surveillances and the Patriot Act applies. I'm sorry."

Bailey laughed. "Knock it off, Gumby. I don't give a fuck about the Patriot Act. I almost invented the SIU. Do you think I don't know professional bullshit when I hear it?"

Gumby was confused and intrigued at the same time. "What?"

"I am retired Mesa PD. I was in the Special Investigations Unit back when it was just sixty guys busting heads."

Gumby was even more confused. He heard of those times. When SIU detectives wrote search warrants on the fenders of their cars... in pencil. When they routinely had shoot-outs... that were never even reported. When bad guys crapped their pants at the thought of being on the secret list of habitual criminals via a mysterious crime computer advanced far ahead of its time... the notorious DD101. "What?"

"Detective. I have spoken with your supervisors. Come to my address, which I will text to you, and pick me up. Secure the bullshit and try not to act like an uptight raggedy-assed two-bit little pussy."

Gumby saw the incoming text. *Frank Bailey?* He wondered. *That can't be THE Frank Bailey.* He said to himself, "How did I not see *this* coming?"

***

Half an hour later he pulled up in front of Bailey's apartment building. Bailey was waiting out front. *He looks like a 1940s private eye,* Gumby thought. *Awesome.*

Bailey hopped in the car. "Detective, I'm Frank Bailey. Sorry for the confusion. I thought they told you." He offered his hand.

Gumby accepted the handshake and replied. "They try not to tell me anything. I have been operating somewhat independently lately."

"Why is that?"

"The Chief hates my guts and wants to transfer me into Accreditation. That's a death sentence for any real cop."

"Agreed. Why does he hate you?"

"I arrest a lot of people."

"From what I've heard about the Chief, that makes sense."

"Can I ask you something?"

"Sure."

"Are you the guy who pushed his dickhead chief in front of a city bus and Homicide covered it up? If so, just blink twice. I understand the statute of limitations."

Bailey involuntarily blinked twice in aggravation after hearing the ridiculous allegation again and then cursed himself for doing it. He attempted to do damage control and explain. "No, of course, not. That's crazy talk. The Chief and I simply had a disagreement, then later that day he had a heart attack and died. I don't know how these rumors get started.

Gumby smiled. "I knew it was true. If anyone asks, I'll stick with the heart attack story. Welcome aboard, Lieutenant. We've never needed you more."

"Right," Bailey said, resigned to the fact that if you kill one chief, you're a chief-killer for life. Even if it never happened.

"You and Father Brannigan being here at the same time is like a sign for better times coming."

"Right."

Bailey, wanting to avoid any more Father Brannigan chatter, tried to get Gumby to focus on the job at hand.

"What's our gig for tonight?"

"We're going to a trailer park off McKellips to buy some meth?"

"We're working narcotics? I thought you were street crime."

"I am. The meth gets me in the door. This piece of shit is a purse snatcher and I'm looking for some stolen purses. He goes for high end stuff. Hermès. I hate purse snatchers. Hey, didn't you shoot…"

Bailey cut him off. "Yeah, I did."

"Awesome."

I should warn you, we might be followed by Jones J. Jones. He's shadowing me for security."

"Big Bad Jones? Good cop. I've worked with him before. He won't interfere unless it gets ugly. And he knows how to do surveillance. We're good."

"Right."

Gumby, to Bailey's dismay, found a way to bring Father Brannigan back into the conversation. "I hear the President assigned Seal Team Six to protect Father Brannigan while he's here. That sounds like overkill to me. But I guess you have Jones, so, that's about the same thing. He's pretty much a one-man special-forces team."

"I've seen him in action. I agree."

They pulled into the trailer park. Gumby found an empty slot in the common parking area that provided a clear view of the target trailer.

The trailer park could have had a neon sign out front that said Meth City, and it wouldn't have been more obvious. The trailers were all in poor condition. Plenty of pit bulls chained up. Quite a few jacked up trucks, a few El Caminos in various stages of restoration, and an abundance of weeds, trash, and debris spread about. An occasional zombie skank did a meth shuffle from trailer to trailer turning tricks, stealing, buying dope, or borrowing something.

Gumby said, "If you look right over there," he pointed out an aging gray trailer with rusty junk cars out front, "you can see the front door. I'll wear a bug so you can listen on channel 15." He handed Bailey his spare radio.

"Thanks. No backup?"

"Nobody available and I want to get this done."

"I'm armed. I can cover you if it gets ugly."

"Thanks, but it should be fine," Gumby stated confidently.

"*It should have been fine* is on a lot of tombstones," Bailey replied forebodingly. He'd had overconfident detectives before. In fact, he'd been one. It comes with a price.

"I got this, lieutenant."

Bailey watched the skinny detective with the goofy outgrown butch haircut, taped Woody Allen glasses, jeans, and Butt Whisker Beer T-shirt walk to the door. He could hear the sound of Gumby knocking on the door through the bug.

A goon answered, at least six-feet-three inches tall and well over two-hundred-and-forty pounds. The man stepped out on the small landing. Bailey could see he had shoulder length dark hair, a red tank top, pajama bottoms, and combat boots. He had full sleeve tattoos on both arms and tattoos on his face. He looked like a giant leaky bag of bad news and malicious intent.

Over the radio he could hear Gumby ask for a teener.

The man invited him in.

The door closed.

Bailey hated trailer parks because the doors were difficult to kick in. You needed a Halligan tool, like the fire department uses, or a big-assed crowbar to crack the door. Bailey had neither on hand in the event of a problem.

He listened over the bug as Gumby and the goon talked. The goon, whose name seemed to be Fanta, negotiated a price.

Fanta must be a street name.

Things seemed calm until Bailey heard those fateful words, "Mesa Police, you're under arrest."

It's a bust! Bailey thought. At least Gumby remembered the magic words better than Slay did.

Then, the sounds of a brawl.

Bailey envisioned the skinny Gumby getting clobbered by the husky goon Fanta, who had to outweigh the scrawny detective by about a hundred pounds. Bailey bailed from the car and ran to the door. It was unlocked. He charged inside to find Fanta face down on the living room floor handcuffed.

"Lieutenant, what are you doing here?" Gumby calmly asked.

"I heard a fight."

"There wasn't a fight. Fanta slipped and hit his head. I'm stabilizing his hands so I can initiate first aid protocols."

"Oh."

Bailey looked around the room and saw a broken lamp, a broken coffee table, blood spatter in three or four locations, what appears to be a tooth on the floor, and a few bags of meth spread about, among other debris that might cause someone who is not highly experienced in undercover work, to mistakenly associate the situation with a fight. Obviously, Fanta just slipped and hit his head. Bailey spotted Jones through the open door, outside in the shadows, ready to react if any meth-head reinforcements showed up.

Gumby said, "Would you watch Fanta while I call for a medic and check the rest of the place, Lieutenant?"

"Sure."

Fanta rolled onto his back and yelled at Gumby, "Who is this old fart knocker, your fucking grandpa?"

Bailey secured Fanta, as asked, by placing a size eleven shoe on his face and pointing his gun at Fanta's nuts. "Get bent, you fucking puke. I'll show you old fart knocker."

Fanta said something else, but the words were garbled. Bailey's foot crushing his mouth and nose like he was grinding out a cigarette butt on a sidewalk interfered with Fanta's diction.

"Got 'em," Gumby shouted from a back bedroom, interrupting Fanta's shoe sole facial.

"What did you find?" Bailey yelled back.

"Stolen luxury purses, four of them. Also, a Rolex and a couple of guns from a local burglary. I think we'll have double-digit felonies waiting for Fanta when we get this all filed.

Bailey smiled and looked down at the suspect. "Ain't that special? Did you hear that, dirtbag? Robbery, burglary, dope dealing, assaulting an officer, disparaging a senior citizen with intent to irritate. Your ass is going away for a bazillion years, pal."

Fanta was desperate. "Wait, I got information!"

Bailey disagreed. "No, you don't."

"Yes, I do."

"No, you don't."

Fanta wiggled around in frustration. "No, dammit, I really do. Listen, I got information. I wanna make a deal."

Bailey was tired of debating the meth dealer. "Detective, he wants to make a deal," he yelled back to Gumby who was still in the other room searching for evidence.

Gumby yelled back, "Ask him if he knows somebody who's a bigger asshole than he is."

Bailed posed the question. "Do you know anybody who's a bigger asshole than you are?"

Fanta frowned. "Is that a trick question?"

"No. Just answer it."

"Well, not bigger in size exactly. But I do know something about the bum murders."

Bailey caught Gumby's attention and waved him back into the room.

"What about the bum murders," Bailey asked, now interested, as Gumby joined them.

Fanta held out. "I'm only talking to Inspector Father Brannigan."

Bailey's heart sank. *Oh fuck! How did this turd hear about Father Brannigan?*

Gumby, being an elite, fast thinking, undercover

operator replied, "Who the hell do you think that is?" He pointed at Bailey.

Bailey's heart sank deeper. *Oh shit... not again!*

Fanta was dubious. "I thought I heard you calling this asshole *lieutenant.*"

"What do you think *inspector* is in Italian, dipshit?" Gumby replied.

Although that didn't make any sense, Fanta, not being a deep thinker, bought it. "Sorry, Father, I didn't recognize you."

Bailey sighed. *What the hell, I might as well go with it.* "I try to remain undercover, my son. Now please, share your information with the detective."

"You don't sound Italian."

Bailey faked an Italian accent that was about as authentic as a bottle of Dollar Store Italian Salad Dressing made in Alabama. "Woulda you-a sound-a like-a n'Italian-a if you was-a undercover, coglione?" Bailey used the only Italian insult word he knew. He wasn't sure he used it correctly. However, he did wave his hands around a lot as he spoke, which legitimized his Italian credentials. After all, Bailey was also once an elite undercover cop and knew how to play a role.

Fanta was sold. "I understand Father. Forgive me. I hoped to cut a deal with these cops, but I only trust you. As soon as I heard you were in town, I was going to give up the street life... in a few weeks."

"Are you Catholic?"

"Yes, Father."

"Then here's your deal, my son, and don't fuck it up. Tell this detective everything, or we send you to the

Vatican for torture until dead, then double secret eternal damnation for one thousand years. Then back to Catholic school for retraining. I'm sorry but it's the best I can do. Pope's honor." *That doesn't sound right,* Bailey thought.

Fanta stiffened and his eyes grew wide. "Fuck!" Not the nuns!"

"It's either that or plead guilty to all this shit you did and do a few years in the joint here in Arizona." Bailey pointed at the meth, bags, and watch. "Take it or leave it." He said firmly.

Gumby weighed in, "Let's face it, dude. A few years in the joint here is a walk in the park for a guy like you. You'd be a big hero inside, the man brought down by the one and only Father Brannigan. I could probably get your name in the paper for this."

Fanta capitulated. "Fine. Just no double secret damnation. I was in Baltimore once and that is as close as I want to get to that shit. And no nuns. I'm left-handed and the penguins beat the living shit out of me with those rulers every day. Did you see the Blues Brothers? That was a documentary!"

I can't believe that shit worked, Bailey thought.

I knew that shit would work, Gumby thought, being more experienced with the modest intellect of the modern new-age local dope dealer and thief culture.

Gumby said to Fanta, "If your information is good, you have your deal. Now talk."

Fanta spilled it. "Here's what I know. I had a customer, a street bummette. She scored a nice chunk of change from pickpocketing a tourist from the east coast. Then she came up here to score. She told me she was leaving town because a man and a woman tried to abduct and kill her the day before, but she was able to escape."

Bailey asked, "Did she say what they looked like? Was it another dealer?"

"No, not at all, it was the opposite. She said they were dressed nice and looked like some kind of businesspeople or something."

Gumby asked, "So what happened?"

"She told me they hit her on the head with a big ass hammer."

Gumby was dubious. "And it didn't kill her?"

"It could have, but it wasn't a good hit. They just grazed her, and it just knocked her ass out for a little bit. When she woke up, she played dead until she could figure out what to do."

Bailey asked, "Then what happened."

"She said they took her someplace where they put on some kind of space suits and had a body bag and everything..." Fanta strained to remember the details. "Uh, it was in a warehouse I think she said. Anyway, she fought them off and escaped. Between her surprising them and their stupid spacesuits being too clunky to move around in, she was able to break away. That's all I know."

"Where is this lady bum now?" Gumby asked.

"Like I said, she left town?"

Gumby took over the questioning in rapid fire sequence. "To where?"

"How should I know?"

"What was her name?"

"Bunny? Sunny? Dunny? Something like that."

"What did she look like."

"White female, thirty, blonde hair, real skinny."

"Can you work with a sketch artist?"

"Why would I?"

"Why not?"

"I got her picture on the camera at the door. I got cameras everywhere man."

Bailey smiled.

***

Half-an-hour later, a patrol unit hauled Fanta away. Bailey, Jones, and Gumby talked as they loaded evidence into Gumby's car trunk.

"You can only imagine my embarrassment when I realized that I didn't spot his cameras," Gumby said.

Jones replied, "Those were stupid cameras. Hidden in the eave spout, his own bathroom, the kitchen. And like a typical meth head, he almost never monitors them anyway."

Bailey added, "Humans always fail their technology. The tech provides convenience, then sloth, then ambivalence, and finally you have biological driven systems failure."

Gumby looked at Bailey with admiration. "That's profound."

Jones was impressed as well. "That's some Steven Hawkings-level stuff, man. You should be hanging with Elon or that YouTube guy instead of us."

"What YouTube guy?"

"The smart one. The guy with the talking fish." Jones looked back and forth at the two, perplexed as to why they didn't seem to know who he meant.

Gumby and Bailey let that one drop.

Gumby said, "No offense, Lieutenant, but you made a terrible Father Brannigan. Not really believable. I'm surprised he bought it. But you pulled it off, so, we should just take the W and never speak of it again."

"I never claimed to be able to fill the shoes of Father Brannigan, Gumby. Who really could? He's a great man," Bailey said, in what he felt was a true demonstration of his excellent undercover acting ability.

Jones said, "Lieutenant Bailey doesn't look anything like Father Brannigan. The Father has a long gray beard, wears dark sunglasses, and has this long black robe thing he wears, sort of like an overcoat, and a big floppy black hat. And he's got that big silver cross thing, like a vampire hunter."

Gumby said, "How do you know that?"

"I caught a glimpse of him at a fight scene for just a split second."

A skeptical Gumby replied, "Are you sure it wasn't Voldemort? Because that's who it sounds like you're describing."

Jones missed both the skepticism and the pop reference. "The Sicilian ice-skater? Why would he be at a bar fight in Mesa, Arizona?"

Bailey asked, "Who?" while also wondering who the hell Voldemort the Sicilian ice-skater was, and why a guy like Jones was following international ice-skating. He seemed like he'd be more of a professional wrestling fan.

A bewildered Gumby uttered a confused, "What?"

Jones answered, lost and unclear himself now, on

what the original question was. "Who?"

Bailey said, "Look, forget all that, uh," He closed his eyes and waved his hands around trying to remember the ice-skater's name, "that volt-meter bullshit. The *important* thing to remember is, I don't look *anything* like Father Brannigan." He refocused the original conversation. "Now, through our amazing detective work, we have obtained a photograph of a person who is very likely the only living eyewitness to the bum murders. That's far more than anyone else in the PD found to this point. But we have to be careful. I believe these homicides are more complex than everyone suspects. There's something deep going on behind them. Perhaps even from within our own. Our having this Meth Chick information could put a target on our backs."

Gumby wasn't surprised. He added, "I predicted all that last week. I venture to guess this is probably the work of one or more psychopaths for direct profit or some type of financial gain operating with the cover of political influence."

Bailey nodded in agreement and thought, *Impressive. Maybe he really is some kind of psychic. Eerie how much he looks like the guy from my squad forty years ago.*

Jones said firmly, "We need to lock this thing down, Lieutenant." He paused, then spoke with a tone of reverence. "With your permission, sir, I request we bring Gumby into the inner circle."

Bailey smiled. This inner circle was starting to sound a lot like an old-time Special Investigations Unit squad. "Of course. I don't see how we can proceed without an experienced undercover detective. Especially one who can peer into the future. Give him a code name and get him a key card to the apartment, which is now officially our command post."

Gumby smiled. "Cool."

Jones put one of his massive paws on Gumby's right shoulder like a cat holding down a dead mouse. "Your code name is Jaguar."

Gumby put his hand on Jones' shoulder, although it was a long reach up for him. He replied solemnly, "I accept this honor."

Jones replied, "Okay, you're in, Jaguar. Call me later and I'll get you a key card. You can't live there full-time like me, Gumby, but that's where we'll meet and do all the top-secret shit."

Gumby asked, "What's *your* code names?"

Jones said, "I'm Buffalo Soldier. The Lieutenant is…"

Gumby cut him off. "He's Blue Moses. I predicted his coming."

Jones and Bailey looked at each other, gobsmacked.

Jones whispered to Bailey, "I told you he could predict stuff."

Bailey whispered back, "Whoa. No one knew that code name but us. You didn't tell anyone?"

Jones looked offended. "Of course not."

Gumby interrupted the whispering. "So, are we going to have challenge coins?"

Jones thought about it. "Yes, but only after we blow the lid off this thing. Until then, we have to be more secret than a preacher's fart during an Easter Sunday sermon. We don't know who we can trust."

Gumby "Got it. I'm in."

Bailey closed the chat. "Let's go 10-8. We have a homicide to clear."

***

Bailey had Jones drive him home since Gumby would be busy for hours tagging evidence and obtaining a sworn statement from Fanta. It was late and Bailey was tired.

Jones asked as he drove. "What's the next step?"

"Tomorrow, I need to try to catch a ride with a Sergeant called Patch. He's a swing shift supervisor. I'm going to try to work a few hours with him. I also have my first meeting with the Review Board at noon."

"Patch is cool. Those board folks are bunch of fuckers, sir."

"So I'm told. But it's just an informal luncheon, no business. They want to get to know me."

"They want to try to intimidate you, sir."

"You're right. Do you want to come as my bodyguard?"

Jones smiled.

Bailey said, "First thing in the morning, we'll get you properly attired."

***

As Bailey and Jones drove home, Elton Maywether, the chairman of the Citizens' Police Review Board, held an impromptu conference call with the five senior board members. "At the luncheon tomorrow, that ex-cop Mayor Henry appointed is going to show up to be introduced. Try to be nice. Also, the Police Chief says he's potentially aggressive and threatening, so as soon as he does something menacing towards us, we file to have him taken off the board."

"File with who?" Gertrude Garza asked?

"I don't know. Somebody. I can rewrite our charter if I have to. The City wouldn't *dare* challenge us. I would go to the media immediately if they did." Elton pointed his nose in the air like indignant royalty, although no one else could see it over the phone.

"So, who is this guy?" Ellen Perrybottom asked. "Does he know I have a doctorate in sociology and that I'm a vegan?"

"I think everyone knows that Ellen" Maywether replied with sarcasm that was lost on the others.

"I'll tell him anyway."

Maywether ignored her and went back to the subject at hand. "He's one of our retired cops. There is a rumor that somehow, he was involved in the assassination of a previous police chief back in the eighties or nineties. So, I suspect he's a white supremist or in some kind of militia. He used to live in Havasu, so that all makes sense, the people there are crazy. Why on earth Mayor Henry would pick such an awful man is beyond me. Henry's black, why would he choose Hitler?"

Ellen piped up. "Oh, I *know* he's a white supremist. He's white, right?"

"Who?" Elton rubbed his forehead. He'd never had a conversation with Ellen in which she listened to anything but the sound of her own voice.

Ellen replied as if she was scolding a preschooler. "This fascist ex-cop you're talking about."

Maywether said, "Oh, yeah, I think so."

"There you have it," Ellen said like an attorney making a point in a closing statement.

"Have what?"

"White supremist."

"Well, *you're* white, Ellen," Gertrude Garza said accusingly. *Does this hippie broad think we can't speak for ourselves?*

"But I'm a woman."

"Barely," Gertrude mumbled.

"What?" Ellen shrieked, clearly triggered.

Gertrude rubbed her sleeve by the phone mic. "I said I can barely hear you. We must have a bad connection. So, what do you want us to do tomorrow, Elton."

"Let's just take a wait-and-see approach. I'm sure he'll do something foolish, and we can respond."

Ellen said forcefully, "Fine. We need to disband the whole police department anyway. They're all white supremacists."

Gertrude replied, "About half of them are women and people of color. What do you call those officers?"

Ellen lowered her voice to a conspiratorial whisper. "The enemy."

The El Sueño Mexican Restaurant.

Maywether was the first to arrive at the luncheon. He checked his watch. He came early to make sure this event went off without a hitch. There was too much riding on this to let anything go astray. Total control was critical. Any retired cop with crazy Lake Havasu opinions had to be kept on a tight leash. He did one more inspection of the venue.

The private meeting room, short hallway down from the main restaurant dining area, was big enough for all ten board members and the new mayor, who previously told Maywether that he wished to drop in and say a few words at the close of the luncheon.

Maywether wanted to have the event somewhere nicer, but this is the only venue who would accept them. Like most Mexican restaurants in the Metro-Phoenix area, the gaudy decorations and furnishings were not like anything one would find typically in Mexico, but the tourists loved it.

It was eleven-forty, and the servers were impatiently waiting with carts of food in the hall.

Ellen Perrybottom and the rest of the board arrived and joined Maywether. Ellen closed her eyes and shook her head. "What kind of person doesn't show up for their welcome luncheon?"

Lucinda Gonzales looked at her watch. "I guess we'll just have to start without him. How embarrassing."

Elton puffed up his chest, as much as a man could pump up a skinny sunken chest. "I agree." The chairman of the Review Board, Elton Maywether, approached the lectern and gaveled the meeting to order.

At that moment, Bailey opened the door. "Sorry, I'm late. I took a few minutes to observe an officer making a traffic stop on the way. I'm Frank Bailey, your new member, commissioner, retired lieutenant, whatever." Bailey could tell by the faces around the table that they didn't give a rat's ass who he was or what he was doing. They wanted to eat burritos and bitch about the police.

Maywether took stock of the older man in the doorway dressed in a dark gray business suit, fancy raincoat, red and blue silk tie, and black 1940s dress hat. He addressed him unenthusiastically, "Welcome to the board, I'm the Chairman, Elton Maywether. Here is your seat, Mister Bailey." He pointed to an empty chair just inside the room."

Still standing in the open doorway, Bailey acted alarmed. "Oh, I can't sit there, Mister Maywether. My back would be to the door. I need to sit over there in the corner. I'll require *her* seat." He pointed to an overweight, heavily tattooed, young, college-age female who looked like she might have murdered her family earlier in the day. "Can you switch with me, toots?" he asked the young woman.

Tattoo woman's face turned red, and she started shaking violently. She began to say something, but Maywether raised a finger. "Just a moment, Serenity."

Bailey thought Serenity might have a stroke.

The rest of the board members were obviously appalled, but Maywether remained calm and quietly asked her to switch seats with Bailey so they could get the meeting started without any further delays.

As soon as she was re-seated, Bailey came further into the room and closed the door behind him. But, to the board's shock, Bailey had Jones J. Jones in tow. Jones, even more stoic than usual, was utterly stylish in the dark blue pinstripe suit Bailey bought him earlier that morning. With a pair of gold framed aviator sunglasses and a snazzy dress hat, Jones looked even more intimidating than usual.

Maywether became visibly upset. "Who is this? We can't bring guests to a board meeting!"

Bailey explained, "Oh, don't worry about Jones. He's my emotional support cop. You see, I witnessed a lot of bad stuff back in the day, and if I suddenly experience a lot of stress over anything, I'll need a pal to calm my chakra. I can't say any more about it. It's an ADA thing. I have a prescription for him."

Bailey didn't really know what a chakra was, but he heard it used by hot chicks in tights on a YouTube video he watched about stretching... for his back pain.

Maywether didn't believe any of that was a real thing. But he couldn't be certain it wasn't. He didn't want to trigger Bailey or say something offensive, especially about a medical condition and start some sort of lawsuit. And especially with that gigantic, scary man standing behind Bailey. He conceded. "Fine. But he can't participate in the meeting."

"Perfect. he doesn't want to," Bailey replied. "Win-Win."

Maywether felt gassy. *This always happens when I'm nervous.* He decided to sit down and tighten his butt cheeks before he let loose with something unpleasant.

Everyone at the square of tables sat silently glaring at Bailey with Jones standing at parade rest behind him as the servers delivered the standard bland meals. Today, a burrito without meat, cheese, or hot sauce at the request of Ellen Perrybottom who insisted the meals be vegan and gluten free. Bailey noticed one of the caterers, an older man, was tying his shoe by the coffee service rather than helping. The man kept his face concealed. He didn't fit in. Then he abruptly left the room, head tucked down, pushing a cart out into the hall.

Odd.

Bailey looked at his plate and decided he wouldn't feed that disgusting mess to a mangy, stray cat, out of respect to stray cats and mange.

Maywether, feeling like he could hold his gas now, called the meeting to order and stood at the tabletop lectern. "Today we are introducing a new board member,

Mister Frank Bailey, who was permanently appointed by the outgoing Mayor. I thought we could perhaps get to know each other today and share some thoughts on the future goals of our board."

Bailey stood, interrupting Maywether's words. "I'll begin."

Maywether was caught off guard. He had a prepared introduction and agenda. "Mister Bailey, if you please..."

Bailey gave him a condescending short bow and then addressed the group. "Thank you, Maywether. I *do* please. First, I don't want to get to know any of you feckless tree-hugging commie knobs."

Tattoo girl clutched her hippy beads and gasped dramatically, "How dare you?"

"And I don't want to hear another word about a future goal. You don't need a future goal. In fact, it's an insult to everything decent in our society that you think you need a future goal. For a committee of this nature to even have a goal, suggests bias, collusion, and corruption of the decision-making process. If you look at the charter, and I have read it carefully, we are directed to act independently, fairly, and objectively in our review of police actions and report our *opinions* to the Mayor, Council, and Chief of Police. To have a goal beyond that is nothing short of a violation of the charter. Thus, I move that this committee, board, whatever, be permanently disbanded for malfeasance and may God have mercy on your souls!"

Ellen Perrybottom shrieked in horror. Maywether ripped a loud, foul, and lengthy fart. Gertrude Garza sat stunned and slack jawed. Tattoo girl started uncontrollably bawling. Bailey noticed she had a long stringy glob of snot hanging off her nose ring like a deflated balloon. It was not flattering.

Bailey and Jones headed for the door.

Lucinda Gonzales, Ellen Perrybottom's life coach, stood defiantly. "You, sir, are a white supremist! I speak for all my people, and my fellow oppressed immigrants when I demand your resignation," she proclaimed defiantly in a heavy Latino accent.

Bailey and Jones stopped in their tracks, looked at each other, then looked at Gonzales. Bailey marched back to the lectern.

Bailey asked, "You're Lucinda Gonzales, right?"

"Si."

"Do these people know your real name is Lucy Kowalski from Pittsburgh?"

She shook in outrage. "Wait... you can't say that!"

Bailey pressed. "Do they know you married and divorced some poor guy named Gonzales twenty years ago and have been playing like you're some kind of oppressed freedom fighter ever since? Your people are Polish, lady. You don't even have kids with Gonzales. I called him. He has lived in Indiana his whole life, at least five generations. He's an Army vet. He has red hair. He doesn't even speak Spanish. And he says you're a nut job."

Her face almost turned purple. "Why I... I resign! I refuse to be insulted like this."

"Insulted? How? Does the truth hurt?" Bailey asked.

Lucinda 'Lucy' Gonzales stomped out of the room shaking with humiliation.

Gertrude Garza covered her face to hide the snicker. *Pinche gringa.*

Bailey didn't know what else to add, so he simply said, "Thank you all so much for this lovely luncheon. I had a swell time. See you at the next meeting." He stepped away from the table, headed for the door, then paused briefly before leaving. In a moment of inspiration, he turned and said, "Oh, by the way, I understand Father Brannigan has a dossier on each one of you." He spun around and headed down the hallway with Jones.

He left the door open behind him. He heard a woman's voice loudly swearing. Or was it two women? Something about being doomed?

Bailey's car

When they were safely back on the street, Jones asked, "Did you practice all that?"

Bailey replied as he drove. "I don't know. I guess I've been thinking about it in my head ever since Hank, I mean Mayor Henry, gave me this stupid job. I felt like it needed to be said."

"Hell yeah, it needed to be said."

"And thanks for the backup, Jones. It really helped."

"Thank you for the suit, lieutenant. I need to dress up more."

"It never hurts to be the best dressed person in the room, Jones. Tacti-cool is fine for the street, but if you want to be taken seriously everywhere else, you have to look the part."

"Copy that. Lesson learned. What's next."

"We get lunch, I couldn't stomach that stupid hippy shit they tried to serve back there. Then, I'll catch a nap before doing a few hours with Sergeant Patch. I think that's what they call him."

"Jim Bob Patch. He's a bad-ass street sergeant. He holds the record for excessive force complaints with no convictions. He's an over-achiever on the street. Chicks dig him, dudes want to be him. Everybody loves that guy, Bailey. He's a cop's cop."

"Good to know. You hungry for anything in particular?"

"I love meat loaf, barbecue, steak, roast beef, burgers, anything red meat based. It's my favorite food group."

"You're a good man. I know a joint that serves a great burger on East Main past Horne and the waitresses all wear gun belts and they have sawdust on the floor. We called it Guns and Buns."

"Sorry, Blue Moses. That place is gone," he said sadly.

Bailey was dumfounded with shock and food grief. "What? What the hell? Did we lose a war?"

"Sorry to be the one who had to break it to you. But don't worry. I know a barbecue place in Chandler that half the family who own it did hard time and they're all heroin addicts or ex-addicts, so you know they make good barbecue."

"Tell me more." Bailey was impressed at the previously unseen enthusiasm Jones was displaying.

"They make a barbecue sandwich that fills a plate spread over a fat Hawaiian bun and a pile of greasy-assed fat French fries on the side. It gave a guy a heart attack once when I was there. He died happy as fuck.

"No kidding?"

"Truth. His last words as he was laying on the ground holding his chest was 'don't try to resuscitate my ass, bitch, just get me one more bite of that motherfucking barbecue!'

"Damn!"

"Hell yeah. That's true as shit. I gave him another mouthful, he chewed that shit and croaked right then and there, happy as hell. I almost cried. It was beautiful."

"No kidding?"

"I had a little cup of barbecue sauce I poured in too. It was the least I could do."

"Then give me the coordinates. This mythical barbecue you speak of might be the only thing that can console me."

The El Sueño Mexican Restaurant.

The new mayor arrived at the meeting expecting a flattering introduction and polite applause. Rather, he found something else. A distressed Maywether, a near-hysterical Miss Perrybottom, and a weeping girl who appeared as if she just escaped from a hippy commune and seemed to have some kind of metal mucus catcher implanted on her nose. *She must have a condition, poor thing.*

The mayor asked, "What the hell happened here? Where is everyone?"

Maywether explained, "We were nuked. Bailey told us all off, basically called us stupid, and then turned our names over to the Vatican."

The mayor was confused. "What?"

Miss Perrybottom stood, "I can't take it anymore. I need to see my therapist." She stormed out of the room.

Maywether said, "I'm sorry. I need to go home and lay down. I don't think I've ever been so triggered. I hate getting yelled at. Bailey is mean." A distraught Maywether followed Perrybottom.

The mayor walked over to the lone survivor, the hippy girl. "Are you okay, Miss?"

She stood up. The mayor tried to give her a consoling hug. She puked on him.

The girl stepped back and wiped her mouth on the tablecloth, then declared, "I quit. I'm moving back to Austin. At least there is culture there."

The puke odor hit the mayor's olfactory nerves, and he puked.

The restaurant manager came in, interrupted the Mayor's heaving, and said to him in a heavy accent, "I'm going to have to charge the city extra for puke clean up, Señor. Two-hundred-dollars."

The mayor flopped his butt down hard on a metal folding chair and cried like a frustrated toddler. "This is the worst luncheon address I ever gave."

In the doorway, the mayor's handlers waited, a tall woman and a short, stocky man.

The woman commented, "He is so pathetically weak."

The man replied, "We need to await direction. But I think he needs to go. We can blame it on any one of those idiots."

She said, "It's almost too easy. Like taking over this city. We stole it and nobody even knows it's gone."

On Patrol

Only an hour into swing shift, Bailey and Patch chatted away like old friends as they cruised the central precinct. Patch pointed out a small sketchy house on a corner lot. "They move dope out of there. Open air drug market somedays. Easy to get a felony bust and information out of this place. It's like they print suspects for us."

"Yeah, the narc-bars on the windows, chained-up pit bulls, trash, dead Bermuda grass, dead palm trees, salty-looking losers loitering around… definitely a home base for party people."

"There used to be only a few of these places we watched, now they're popping up everywhere."

"In my time, they took over multiple blocks of territory."

"What did you do?"

"Took it back and bulldozed them."

"No shit?"

"Did you ever hear of the Gambling Shack or Little Mexico?"

"No."

"And you never will."

"Damn."

"Yeah, somewhere I still have photos of the bulldozers coming in and leveling those places. We went scorched earth with jumps and search warrants. Then our admin narcs got them declared nuisances and filed civil suits and RICO cases against the owners. More often than not, a lot of those places were owned by the cartels."

"Wow. We're lucky to get *any* support from the courts or City Hall now."

"I have no doubt you guys are doing the same stuff we are. It's just tough without getting any backup from above. We had quite a few years of public support and political support. It makes all the difference."

The conversation paused while Patch checked off on a traffic stop. Bailey checked his email while Patch dealt with a local mom speeding twenty-five over the limit to pick up her kid at an after-school sports event. There was a message from Slay: *we should talk.* Bailey sensed it was time for more than just another one-on-one chat.

When Patch came back to the car, Bailey said, "Do you know much about the bum murders?"

"Yeah. I might have a source. Why?"

"Try to get off work early and come to my place tonight. I'm going to have some people you know over. It will prove interesting."

"No problem. What time?"

"Around nine."

"I'll be there."

Bailey sent out a flurry of text messages.

The Mayor's Office

The Mayor sat behind his desk, still upset about being vomited on. *It had to be on that Tom Ford suit my out-of-state donor gave me,* he thought. *The cleaners will never get the puke odor out.*

His primary aides were out dealing with a zoning crisis. The only people on the floor were his receptionist and the two scary creeps everyone called *the handlers,* a tall, thin woman and some short, stocky man. They weren't exactly bodyguards, but they *did* do some bodyguard stuff. They weren't advisors either, but he found himself often doing exactly what they told him to do. They weren't even on the city payroll. They worked for his donor, rumored to be some New York hedge fund guy who was interested in the city.

The mayor's mind drifted. *If I'm being honest with myself, I should have never taken this job. I have no idea what the hell I'm doing. I hate this town. But if I do my term, I get a job in Washington D.C. as a lobbyist. I have to get a grip... but the stress!*

The intercom buzzed. It was the receptionist. "Call on line one, sir."

"Who is it?"

"A reporter. She needs a comment on the Father Brannigan investigation."

"What? That's not a real thing."

"Yes, it is. I saw it on TV," the receptionist said, surprised that the mayor would suggest that Father Brannigan wasn't real.

"I'm not taking any calls. No comment. There is no Brannigan!"

"But the Pope sent him." She was like a terrier with a dead rodent. She wouldn't let it go. She went ahead and connected the call anyway out of spite.

The mayor, now angry, yelled into the phone, "The Pope can blow it out of his...!"

Cara Carter, channel nine news anchor and local Emmy award winning journalist replied, "Is that your quote, Mister Mayor?"

"Wait, wut?"

The infamous reporter with the infamous cleavage kept the pressure up. "I didn't have an opportunity to tell you that this interview is recorded, but you are a public official, so I have a right to record it anyway. So, you're cooked, bud. Is there anything further you would like to add."

"You can't print that!"

"I work for television news. We don't print things. We broadcast them to over a million homes across Arizona. And by the way, I've seen your type my entire career. You act like your better than everyone else, but I think under that squeaky clean persona is a real stinking dirtbag."

"What?"

"Did I mention that I'm Catholic?"

"I...I... uh... I apologize!" The Mayor pleaded.

She ignored his obviously fake contrition. "Thank you for your time, Mister Mayor. We will be reaching out to Father Brannigan for his response."

"You mean he's real?"

"Of course he's real. We're the news. We have sources."

"Oh no."

"Oh yes."

The Mayor slammed the phone down and stomped out to the reception desk. "Why did you put that call through?" he screamed at the receptionist.

"You told me to, sir," she replied with a straight face. She, like every other long-term city employee, hated the mayor's guts.

"No, I didn't. I will have you fired."

"Yes, you did. And if you try to fire me, I'll go to HR about your little fling with that city librarian in your office I walked in on last month. I was traumatized."

"What? That was nothing."

"You had your pants off, sir."

"It was hot out that day."

"Was he hot too?"

"I can explain. That wasn't what it looked like."

"It was exactly what it looked like."

"He was off duty."

"Not all of him. Is HR, my next stop, sir?"

"Fine. Forget it. I know how to deal with this. Hold all of my calls." The mayor stomped out of the office and went home. He really didn't know how to deal with *any* of it.

The receptionist posted an all personnel announcement stating the Office of the Mayor was closed for the day. Then she closed the blinds on the office's front windows, turned on some music, and ordered a mobile manicure service and a Frappuccino delivery on the Mayor's personal credit card. *It's not my fault that creep didn't notice his wallet fell out of his pants pocket on one of his little library worker peccadilloes. My silence comes with a stout fee.*

Bailey's Apartment

By nine-thirty that evening the small ad hoc group of elite investigators assembled for the first time in Bailey's apartment. Bailey's twelve-hundred-square-foot apartment home was unusually large for the typical two-bedroom high-rise residence, leaving plenty of room for mingling and drinks as the team enjoyed the sprawling view. The evening air was warm enough to leave the patio doors open, creating more of a cocktail party ambiance, rather than a murder investigation briefing.

Patch whispered to Slay, "This place looks like a rum bar I visited in Miami one time."

Bailey heard the comment. "That's by design. I like the vibe. My dream is to spend my remaining days on the Florida coast. Coffee in the morning, mojitos in the evening. Walks on the beach and floating in the water in between."

Jones looked at Bailey intently. "Respect."

Gumby added, "Agreed."

Ma Donna asked the first question while she took it upon herself to assume command of the kitchen and distribute drinks, coasters, and napkins to everyone. "So why are we all here, Lieutenant."

"Take a seat and I'll explain."

The group made themselves comfortable in the dark black and brown leather couch, chairs, and padded leather bar stools.

Bailey stood in front of the sliding patio doors, the open night sky behind him, and began. "First, you were all selected by Mayor Henry, my old partner on the PD. He holds each of you in the highest regard."

The group was visibly humbled at the endorsement. Mayor Henry had earned their respect as well.

"Secondly, we all want the bum murders solved. These poor homeless homicide victims are pawns in something bigger. I can feel it. Their murders are an abomination against civilized people. I want justice and I think each of you do too."

Everyone nodded in agreement.

"Third, for reasons unknown, and perhaps even for nefarious purposes, none of the information on the bum murder cases is being released or shared, effectively crippling any momentum on the case."

Patch muttered, "You got that right."

Bailey continued, "And last, but not least, if *we* don't

blow the lid off of this thing, no one else will. So, I am forming this irregular work group to do an off-the-books, totally unauthorized, probably illegal parallel investigation into these murders. We all have our own resources. It's time we share them."

Those words received a round of applause, then the officers hopped up and surrounded Bailey, patting him on the back and thanking him. Ma gave him a big matronly kiss on the cheek.

Jones put a hand up and commanded attention. "I got something to say." He made eye contact with each team member before turning his attention to Bailey. "We have a big leadership void on our PD. Ever since that new chief came in from out of town, nothing has been about police work. It's been all politics and social justice. All we want, all we need, is a chance to do our jobs. Protect the citizens, throw the fear of God into bad guys, and serve the public. We just want to be cops again."

The others looked at Jones in amazement. None of them had ever heard him say more than a couple of words a day in the years they had known him, let alone such an articulate and heartfelt speech.

Jones felt their reverential stares and responded. "And all you guys suck."

That comment garnered some laughs as Bailey told everyone to sit back down. "Listen, we're going to do this like old school cops. Collect the evidence, squeeze the confessions, and finally submit the case while staying invisible. We need to put it all together and drop it into the right hands at the right time. So, we'll go around the room and share a quick overview what we each have, then make our assignments. Is everyone good with that?"

The group all gestured and mumbled agreement.

Bailey picked up a shopping bag from behind a chair in the corner. "Here are some burner phones. I have one for each of you and a couple of spares. We can use these in case our phones ever get subpoenaed. Everyone exchange numbers and put them in your phones under your code names. Everybody write your number on this pad." He tossed a yellow pad onto the coffee table. "Then pass it around again and load them up at the end of the meeting. Jones will set up a group text we can use to share emergency information."

"Jaguar is better at that than I am, Blue Moses."

"Who the hell are you talking about?" Slay asked.

Jones said, "Code names."

"*We* don't have code names," Patch complained, a little more emphatically than one would expect an adult to object to not have a secret code name.

Ma jumped in, "Yeah, why *don't* we have code names?"

Bailey raised a hand to turn back the impending code name tsunami before it got out of control. "We'll get to that later. That's the *end of the meeting* thing I just mentioned. While you guys are jotting numbers, let's start with Patch."

Patch stood. "I have a buddy in homicide. Well, he *was* in homicide until the Chief kicked him out this week. Ronny Cortez."

Ma interjected, "Ronny is good people."

The group again mumbled in agreement.

Patch continued, "Yeah, he is. He's as frustrated as the rest of us. These cases have a distinctive M.O. It looks more like the perp is some fool and/or fools unknown who learned about serial killers on a cable TV detective series. It's over the top and it's stupid." Patch began spitting out details of the method of operation. "Hammer hit to the forehead, stripped, soaked in bleach. Body abandoned naked by a dumpster. No DNA or useful evidence. Always in the central corridor of the city. I feel like there is a reason someone is doing this, but it isn't a mental case degenerate maniac. I saw a scene, or at least a glimpse of a scene. Maybe I can add more as we talk."

Bailey was taking notes. He looked up and said, "Good. That's really good. Who's next?"

Ma related the story of Sky Hump spilling his guts to her and Bailey, laying out the details of his information. "After I got him back in an interview room at the jail, I went upstairs to get one of my squad mates to help with the interrogation, and by the time I got back, he's gone. They tell me he was lawyered up, and someone ordered him transported to County Jail. I couldn't get any answers to who moved him or who ordered it. How does somebody intervene like that on an active felony case? So, this whole, *send a message* thing sounds like a problem from within the city, maybe within the PD."

Slay said glumly, "It's starting to smell that way."

Gumby added his report. "We have a photograph. This person was abducted by the killers. If we find her. We have a witness." He shared the details as told by Fanta as he handed out copies of the best photo they had from Fanta's cameras. "She goes by something like Bunny, Sunny, or Dunny. That's probably her street name. She's a white female, thirty, blonde on that day, and thin build. From the photo analysis we think she is about five-foot-five. She's a pickpocket, addict, prostitute, and she's available for a reasonable price if you are lonely and can find her. Penicillin sold separately."

Everyone snickered. Dark humor is the only therapy that prevents good cops from going off the rails.

Patch was still chuckling at Gumby's analysis but noticed that other than what might have been a small hiccup, Jones expression never changed. The big man looked as grim as if he just found mouse turds in his breakfast cereal. Patch whispered back, "Get a grip, Jones. You're going to embarrass yourself. Calm down."

"Sorry Patch. Gumby is hilarious. I just lost it for a minute."

Slay spoke next. "That's interesting. I worked my department connections and some snitches. I had the theory that there is a financial element to this. Someone is acting out. Patch is right. This isn't a psychotic pervert. This is someone trying to make us think it's a psychotic pervert." Slay fumbled around in his messenger bag and retrieved a document. "Here is a list of every murder with date, location, time discovered, estimated time of death. If we had some surveillance camera shots, we might have the suspects."

Ma said, "Definitely, store cams, traffic cams, even the license plate readers on some of the patrol cars in the area. Why don't we have that?"

Patch stood up. "We don't have it because someone at City Hall doesn't *want* us to have it. I wasn't going to say anything because I don't want to risk burning a source, but I have reason to believe that since the new assistant city manager was appointed, a few new faces showed up at City Hall, and they're bad news. That might be our nexus."

Bailey said, "I met the Chief. He's a patsy. That guy is too stupid to put together any kind of a conspiracy. I haven't met the new Mayor."

The group shared a chuckle.

"He's cut from the same cloth, Lieutenant," Slay said. "A goof. Seems like he was placed there for a good reason, or a bad one."

The team seemed to agree.

Gumby said softly what the other team members were thinking. "We need Father Brannigan on this case."

Ma, Slay, and Patch enthusiastically supported that statement with toasts and grunts of approval. Bailey felt an urge to come clean, but he fought it back.

Jones disagreed. "We don't need Father Brannigan. He's busy fighting those Vatican demons that showed up in the jail. That's his job. We got to fight our own demons. We can't ask him to do our job too."

Ma asked, "What if they're the same demons?"

Jones replied, "Then he'll find us."

Bailey saw his opportunity to shut down the Brannigan chat, at least for the time being. "Jones is right, you guys. Father Brannigan is *definitely* too busy for this. He's on special assignment for a reason. We need to fix this ourselves."

The obviously disappointed cops reluctantly agreed.

Bailey added, "I just wish we had a wild card."

Gumby the prognosticator said with his quirky use of the language, "Be patient, sir. I would venture to guess if we need one, one shall arrive."

Bailey didn't know what to do with that, so he went into Lieutenant mode and gave some orders. "Find the girl. Figure out the financial scam. If it is local, then someone local will know. We'll have victims on the financial side already, although they might not even know they are victims yet. Figure it out. We meet here again two nights from now. Does that work?"

The team agreed to the plan.

Gumby said "I'm going to work my street contacts. I've rarely seen an addict claim they were leaving town who made it more than two miles. That Meth Chick is findable."

Bailey thought about that a moment then replied, "If you find her, just watch her and call us. If someone at the PD stole Ma's snitch, they'll steal Meth Chick too. Maybe I can find one of my old crew and, with some unofficial cover from you and Jones, we can put the bag on her and take her somewhere for questioning."

Slay said half-heartedly, "Isn't that kidnapping, Lieutenant?"

"Not if you have love in your heart and justice in your soul, Slay. Then it's called community policing."

Slay seemed satisfied with that answer, not that he had a problem with well-intentioned extra-judicial kidnappings in the furtherance of justice.

Ma added, "I'll have a look at the financial motives. There's a local CPA firm that was burglarized. We recovered everything for them and made an arrest. They do a lot of work on downtown projects. I have a strong connection with the owner there. She'll keep her mouth shut. I trust her."

Patch and Slay offered up some contacts they would work at Homicide.

Jones stood and announced, "We all need code names. I already set up a text thread. You're all in it. I'm Buffalo Soldier. The Lieutenant is Blue Moses. Gumby is Jaguar."

Patch said, "I'm Geronimo."

"Because you're Native American?" Gumby asked.

"That, and I was a paratrooper. It's why I can't chase bad guys very well. Bad knees."

"Cool."

Slay claimed the codename, Captain.

Jones asked, "Why do you want to be called Captain?"

"It's the only way I'll ever make Captain, unless I buy a boat."

Gumby said, "We don't even have Captains anymore. They made them all commanders about a million years ago."

Ma added, "They desecrated our culture when they pulled that lame bullshit."

The group expressed unanimous agreement.

Patch said, "That name might get confusing. We should call you Captain Chaos. That sounds bad ass."

A metaphorical light bulb came on over Slay's head. "I like that... but just Chaos. Switch mine to Chaos."

Bailey jotted it down. "Fine. Ma?"

"Ripley."

Patch asked, "The outer space movie Ripley, or the Believe it or not one?"

"Of course it's the outer space Ripley."

Jones said, "Cool. Space Marine. Didn't she have a cat?"

That question out of nowhere made Ma do a long blink before answering. "I don't think so, Jonesy."

"Buffalo Soldier."

"Uh, yeah. Buffalo Soldier.

Bailey got them back on track. "We had a good briefing, people. Now, hit the streets. This old-timer needs to get his forty-winks in. See you here two nights from now."

They said their goodbyes and disappeared into the night. All that remained in the apartment was Jones and Bailey. They had a quiet nightcap on the patio.

Jones said, "I'm pretty sure Ripley had a cat."

Bailey replied, "I don't know, Jones. I can't remember. It's been a long time since I've seen that movie. All I know is that I don't have a cat. Now let's turn in. I'm beat."

"I'm going to do five-hundred push-ups first to relax, then I'll turn in, sir."

"That, or a cup of tea. Whatever works for you. Good night, Jones."

Bailey retired to his room. He had a strange feeling. A good feeling. He felt like a cop again.

***

In the parking lot outside of Bailey's apartment, an older man in a hotel server uniform sat in his car fumbling with the long-range laser listening device he built with plans from Grok and parts from eBay. He was able to pick up enough from eavesdropping on the briefing to know his own next steps. "Wild card?" he said to himself. "Yeah, that sounds about right."

CHAPTER 9

Offices - Century Private Accounting LLC

Ma Donna sat patiently in the reception area waiting for the owner of the accounting firm to come out of her office. She saw the skinny woman at the front desk trying to steal surreptitious glances at her as she waited. *She either isn't used to cops being in here or she has a traffic warrant.*

After a five-minute game of peek-a-boo with the receptionist, Ma saw the owner come out as she escorted a client to the door. After the owner finished her polite farewells, she smiled and greeted Ma.

"Nice to see you again, Detective. Please come on back."

Ma exchanged a polite greeting and followed the woman to her office.

"So how can I help you?"

"I don't know if you can," Ma confessed. "I'm looking for something that I'm not sure exists and I don't know where to begin."

"A police matter?"

"Yes."

The accountant smiled. "Let's begin with the numbers."

"What kind of financial benefits would come from a

string of homicides in downtown Mesa, and who would receive them."

The accountant made a face like she just heard her favorite stock crashed as she scooted back in her chair.

"Is this the homeless murders?"

"Yes."

"And this is confidential?"

"Absolutely. I was never here."

"You know I sit on a few boards around the city. And I also have a few real estate investments downtown."

"Right. That's why I came to you."

"I was approached by two so-called city workers with a bid to buy all my local holdings in the downtown area for a ridiculously low price."

"When?"

"Four months ago."

"Who?"

"A man and a woman. The man looked like a little short muscle guy, like a gym rat. The woman was very tall and thin. They seemed... odd."

"How so?"

"They didn't really represent anyone to my knowledge. They claimed to be from the city, but they also said there were buyers working with a city project to redevelop a significant chunk of downtown. Some public and private sector joint initiative."

"Is that true?"

"I don't think so. I suspect it's total bullshit."

"So, what happened?"

"Nothing. Except these dead bodies started turning

up. Then I lost my renters. I can't find new renters. The property values are dropping. It's crazy. A lot of the homeless and the local criminals seemed to have moved on at the same time. You'd think if the criminals left, property would go up and there would be more of a positive pop to residential and commercial real estate. But, no. It's the opposite. And it happened fast. Extraordinary situation. It's impossible this happened randomly."

"The big question is why."

"Yeah. Someone probably wants every piece of property downtown for some reason. I'm going to have to dump my holdings if I can't put renters in them. My realtor showed them a few times, but the people always backed out, never explaining why. I can't even get government assisted housing tenants right now. That was cut off."

"Interesting. Now, next question. Who?"

"I think it has something to do with the new Mayor and maybe someone in City Hall. They have to have someone in the City Manager's office. Maybe an assistant city manager. It's big. I don't get it. Mesa isn't exactly turning the downtown area around yet and probably never will unless they move all the social services to the freeway corridor and turn Country Club Drive into a connector freeway to the 101 and the 60."

"Ha, strong opinions. Sounds like you've given that some thought."

"I forgot to add bulldoze the trolley line. It's a money pit."

Ma laughed. "Yeah, but it does help the prostitutes and drug dealers get from downtown Phoenix to downtown

Mesa, so we have that going for us."

The accountant smiled. "None of that can ever happen. Too many obstacles. But I hope someone has a better idea and the moxie to pull it off, whatever it is. It's potentially a beautiful little downtown."

Ma was satisfied she had enough, but there was still one more question. "Any names we can apply to this theory?"

"No. No names. Just that man and woman. That's the only starting point I have. If they're connected to this real estate angle, there is your clue."

Ma was satisfied. "Thank you. This helps a lot."

"Anytime I can assist, please let me know."

The two women shook hands and Ma left.

In the parking lot, Ma scanned the area and checked the back seat before getting in her car, as by habit. She paused a minute to gaze over towards the center of town. *Finally, some potential motive.*

Bailey's Apartment

Bailey was sipping his first cup of coffee of the morning and reviewing his notes when Jones came back in.

"Sir, your building's gym doesn't have weights that go over three hundred pounds. I'll have to walk over to the headquarters gym. Will you be okay?"

"Sure, Jones. I was actually going to complain about that gym thing before you moved in." Bailey lied. "It's ridiculous."

"I know. How is a man supposed to keep in shape?"

"Right."

Jones left again. Bailey went back to scratching down ideas with his mechanical pencil and researching.

He did a web search, made some calls, and was able to rent some warehouse space short term over the phone. It was in a small commercial facility near Falcon Field. Bailey figured it might serve as a good place to take Meth Chick for questioning if they found her, assuming they found her after regular business hours and assuming he could find another retiree willing to risk a prison sentence for one more shot at breaking a big case.

Finding another guy is going to be a problem. Most of them from my era are deceased or in poor health, part of the price one pays for being a good cop. It takes a physical toll on the human body. Who is left?

Bailey went through his roster of old co-workers.

Blaster? No, I wouldn't know where to begin to find him. And he is uncontrollable anyway. His middle name is insubordination.

Pappy? I don't know where he is either.

Jack? He'd be willing, but then we'd have every woman we ran across hitting on him... or vice versa. And he'd probably shoot somebody, just because. He's old, but he still has game. No, he'd get us all arrested.

Maybe some of the troopers I used to work with, or other guys from the task force operations?

Jeff? He's in good shape and available, but his answer to every problem is a belt-fed machine gun. Living in Cave Creek will do that to a man.

Mongo? We're only up against a massive murder conspiracy led by some cut-throat psychopath serial killers. Releasing Mongo back on the street would be overkill, even at his age. Again, too much.

Things were different in the eighties. These guys were just normal cops back then. Dirty Harry was just a boring documentary to us.

Who is an excellent goon? Because this is going to be goon work.

Then he realized he really didn't want to risk anyone else's golden years doing something as stupid as what he had planned. Bailey was ready to spend the rest of his life in prison or to die working a case. There wasn't anything new for him to look forward to. Everything good in life for him was in his rear-view mirror. He couldn't drag any of those fellow officers he loved from the old days into his current drama and live with himself. They all have someone. They still have a life.

This is what happens when you're old and alone.

As he thought about those glory days gone forever, loneliness, and time passing by way too fast, he felt depression wrapping its tentacles around him and squeezing. He knew it what it was. It almost had him once before, after retirement. He knew it was irrational. But it was the most real thing in the world when it happens. This was the first time he felt a breakdown coming since he left Havasu. He got up to pour some more coffee, hoping to fend the darkness off. *The cold blue darkness. I know what you are.*

Then there was a knock at his door. *Probably one of the detectives with an update.* He splashed some cold water on his face in the kitchen sink and dried with a dish towel.

He opened the door to an eyeful of boobs, hair, and a short purple dress that should have been worn at a ballroom gala rather than in the hallway of his apartment building. He blinked. There was a cameraman behind the woman.

Microphone in hand, the woman blasted him with information. "I'm Cara Carter from Channel Nine News. I've been following the Father Brannigan story, and from the proceedings of the recent Police Review Board meeting, I believe you have spoken to him. I also believe you can add information to my investigation. We'll only need about an hour of your time. May we come in?"

The woman began to force her way through the doorway with the cameraman snugged in behind her like a vampire bat.

Bailey was rarely taken by surprise. He pushed them away instinctively, placing his right palm out, unintentionally arriving somewhere slightly above and between the area of the reporter's epic cleavage, while pulling the Glock 26 out of his bathrobe pocket with the left and jamming it into the cameraman's forehead.

"Stop right there!"

It happened fast. The cameraman, a local news agency professional who had covered everything from campus protests to traffic accidents, wet his pants a little. Cara shrieked and leaped backwards. The reporter and cameraman collapsed into a heap.

Bailey realized as he looked at them sprawled out on the hallway floor, they were harmless. He calmly said, "Sorry, I've only had one cup of coffee this morning. Now, what is it you wanted again?" He put out a hand to help the reporter up.

The cameraman asked, "May I use your bathroom, sir?"

"Sure, as long as you turn your camera off and leave it

by the front door."

He replied obediently, "Yes, sir," and meekly got to his feet, took off his rig and set the camera inside the doorway, and walked back to the restroom to clean himself up.

"Would you like some coffee?" Bailey asked Cara.

"Thank you," she replied, now more amused and intrigued than shocked or angry.

Bailey yelled at the bathroom door. "Rinse out the spot in the sink. It's okay to use the hair dryer to dry it."

From behind the door the acquiescent cameraman said, "Thank you, sir."

Cara asked, "Does this happen often?"

"Oh, not really. Just a delivery guy, the property manager, and some random guy trying to sell a bottled water delivery service. But I've only been here about eight weeks, so there will probably be more. It's better if they come in the afternoon, but what ya gonna do?"

Cara chuckled at the thought of so many visitors getting a gun shoved into their face. "I'll always remember to call first."

"A very good idea." He poured her a cup of coffee and directed her to the patio to sit down and chat. "So, how can I help you, Cara."

"First of all, from what I heard, you set that preposterous police review board on their ear. I say, bravo!"

Bailey laughed. "That surprises me. I thought all reporters loved that community board anti-cop stuff."

"Not me. I'm thinking about retiring and maybe running for local office. I'm sick of these two-faced pukes."

"Retiring? You can't be close to that age."

"Good genes. I'm fifty-seven and I've planned my finances well. I can do whatever I want."

"Well, congratulations. And I'm glad to hear you aren't part of the defund the police crowd."

"My grandfather was a cop in New York, back in the old days. I've always been pro-police."

"Interesting." *Is there a little chemistry here? Can't be.*

"Look, I apologize for the strong entrance. We had that welcome of yours coming. It's just how we steam roll these people to get the truth. But I see now that it was improper with you." She became serious and took a more professional tone. "Not to waste any of your time, Mister Bailey, I'm here to learn about the Father Brannigan story. I heard you referenced him at that meeting."

"Off the record?"

She grinned. "This time, and this time only."

Bailey felt his heart race. *What a smile.* "Let me come clean then. I just said that to mess with those pretentious knobs. To be honest, I'm not even sure Father Brannigan really exists."

An aura of desperation fell over Cara. "I *really* hope he exists. I staked my reputation on it. It was a foolish move, but the station is trying to force me out. Partly because of my political opinions and partly because of age. They need a new *hot chick reporter* in front of the camera for ratings. Or at least that's what the rumor is. Father Brannigan was my Hail Mary play."

Bailey felt bad. His playing around with Possum Momma had unforeseen repercussions, including Cara possibly losing her job. Bailey decided to go out on a limb and possibly forge an important new ally. "Perhaps if I break a big story, not saying I will, and you get an exclusive, maybe they'll keep you on."

She was intrigued. "What kind of big story?"

She put her hand on Bailey's leg. Old or not, he was about to embarrass himself. He stood up to get more coffee, although his cup was still full.

He talked as he walked to the kitchen. "There's something going on in town. It's too soon to say with any certainty, but I think it's big. I might have something for you in a couple of days. Can you let me off the hook for now? My word is good on this."

She was skeptical. "Not that I don't believe you, but it's in my reporter DNA to ask. *How* big?"

"Public corruption and murder big."

Cara was impressed. "Deal."

She stood up and followed him to the kitchen. "By the way, how old are you, Bailey?"

"Is that newsworthy?"

"Just curious."

"I'm seventy-one." *When I say that out loud, that sounds like a hell of lot of years.*

She said playfully, "You know, you're not too badly preserved for an old dinosaur."

He laughed. "Thanks, Cara. Somedays I feel like a hundred."

"So, are you saying you're too old for dinner tonight?"

Bailey almost dropped his coffee cup. "Like a date?" *I didn't see that coming.*

"Yeah. Like a date."

"Cara, I just became a widower a little over four months ago. I'm not sure it's time."

"It's just dinner, Bailey. I'm not proposing."

He thought about it for a long moment. "If I can buy, we have a deal."

"Then it's the Compass Grill at eight."

"Compass grill? Then you're buying."

They stared at each other for a full five seconds, each wondering if the other was serious, before breaking up in light laughter. Bailey squeezed out words between chuckles, "I'm kidding. I love that place. It would be a pleasure to have dinner with you, Cara. Should we meet there?"

"Perfect. It's close to the studio. I can head over right after I finish with the evening broadcast.

The cameraman came out of the bathroom. "What's so funny?"

Cara said, "A retired cop and a reporter walked into a bar..."

"What?" The cameraman, like a lot of techies, did not have a well-developed sense of humor and the conversation was less convivial before he went in the bathroom, leaving him confused.

Cara waved him off. "We were just kidding around. We're good here, buddy. Let's head over to City Hall and rain on their parade." She helped him load his backpack of recording gear.

"He's not going to shoot us in the back, is he? The cameraman asked as he edged for the door, still a bit nervous about how their host greeted them.

"Not today," she said. "Probably." Then she winked at Bailey who gave the cameraman have a half-hearted death stare and pointed a finger gun at him. The man turned and scurried down the hall to the elevator, hoping never to see Bailey again.

At least the poor kid didn't wet his pants this time, Bailey thought.

"See you later," Bailey said as he saw Cara out.

Cara smiled. "Looking forward to it. And if you *do* hear anything real about Father Brannigan, please give me a call."

Having a reporter on my ad hoc squad might give us the edge we need if things get ugly. I'll bring it up with the team next meeting.

"Will do." Bailey gave her a thumbs up and closed the door.

Just when I was beginning to think all hope was lost, hope knocked on the door looking for me. Sorry, the cold blue darkness can't have me today. Not yet.

***

When Jones returned from the gym, showered, and dressed, the pair left to take a look at the bum murder crime scenes and see what was there that the Chief didn't want anyone else to know. Bailey let Jones drive, although the big man didn't fit well behind the wheel of Bailey's C-Class Mercedes.

"Lieutenant, if we stop for lunch, I might not be able to squeeze back in here. I'm one tater-tot away from not fitting."

"Maybe you're just claustrophobic, Jones. Have you ever been diagnosed for that? The dealer says a large person should be comfortable in this car."

"Was the dealer who told you that a great big son-of-a-bitch like me?"

"Well, no."

"Give me his name later. I'll shove his dumb ass in the glove compartment and explain how there is plenty of room in there for a full-grown man."

"Maybe we should use your Excursion next time."

"Maybe we should."

The team had put together a fairly complete crime map of the known locations where the bodies were found. Bailey created a copy in his notebook and broke it down into grids. No one except homicide knew where the murders occurred, and it was unclear if even homicide knew either. Bailey and Jones inspected every spot on their map in the course of three hours.

"You know what I'm seeing when I look around this area, Jones?"

"What?"

"Abandoned houses, vacant lots, and empty commercial structures."

"Yeah."

"And in the center, that church."

"The Catholic church?"

"Yeah."

"It's pretty run down too."

"Let's see if anyone is home and talk to them."

"I wished I would have worn my new suit now, Lieutenant. I didn't know we were going to church."

"It's okay. We're on a special mission, like Father

Brannigan, only Mesa PD instead of the Vatican. It's almost the same thing."

"Then I'm in."

Inside the aging church they found Father Garcia mending pews with a few simple hand tools. A lone parishioner, an older slender man who kept his head down, sat in the far corner pew in the back.

Bailey addressed the priest. "Father, I'm Frank Bailey. This is my colleague, Jones. Could we speak to you a few minutes about a crime problem in the area?"

"Crime? That's about all that's left. The good people are gone or are leaving. Please, come back to my office and we can talk."

Bailey and Jones followed the old priest into a small combination library and office in the back of the church.

"So, how can I help you Mister Bailey?"

"Father, I've noticed the areas in these grids are almost devoid of homes and businesses. In fact, they're like a no-man's-land." Bailey showed the priest the map he created in his notebook.

The priest examined the map and agreed. "Yes, I must concur, Mister Bailey. This was a poor, but thriving, neighborhood just six months ago. Then these murders began. First the homeless were gone, then the residents started selling out or moving. The landlords tell me the homes that are left are un-rentable. No one knows why."

"Do you have a guess?"

"Yes. Someone wants to buy everyone out and do something with this land. I don't know what, though. They want my church too. That will give them this entire area." The priest pointed out a large rectangular sector of the south-central core of the city. "There is something here. They want it at any cost."

"So, someone approached you?"

"Yes. A man and a woman. They claimed to be from the Mayor's office. They made a cash offer. Of course, I can't sell this property. It's not mine. I referred them to the Diocese. That was the last I heard of it. That is until a week ago."

"What happened a week ago?"

"I received a notice from the Archdiocese that this property was going to be sold at auction in three months and I needed to vacate. They mentioned something about an assignment in Nogales. Now, no one returns my calls or even talks to me." The old man hung his head.

Bailey put a comforting hand on his shoulder, "Are you *sure* it was the Archdiocese?"

"Well, I assume so. It was someone I had never heard of before, but they seemed to know all the details of the church."

Bailey pulled his leather notebook out of his jacket pocket and scribbled down his name and phone number. He tore out the page and handed it to the priest. "Call me if you think of anything or if someone contacts you that you do not feel good about."

Jones pulled out a business card. "And if you get scared or anyone threatens you, call me. And then get ready for an emergency confession after I straighten it out."

The priest smiled at the joke. Then he realized Jones wasn't joking.

"Yes, my sons. Thank you. I will reach out if something happens. Thank you for coming by. It's a blessing to know there is someone out there watching. I prayed for this."

Jones said, "It's okay, we know about Father Brannigan. We're not working directly with him, but we are on the same page."

Bailey cringed. *What ever happened to the Jones who never says two words? He hasn't shut up since this case started.*

Father Garcia smiled. "Father Brannigan has not yet called me. But we are grateful he is here. I was shocked that the Vatican would send someone to Mesa. It is a mystery."

Bailey felt a hint of stomach acid. *Did I do this? Does he really believe in Father Brannigan? Well, crap! I'm going to hell and I'm not even Catholic. It's time to get out of here.*

Bailey said, "Father, my colleague and I will be taking our leave now. Like I said, please call if you need us."

"Bless you, my sons."

Bailey and Jones shook his hand, thanked him, and left. He noticed the lone man who was sitting in the back of the church was gone.

Outside, Bailey asked Jones, "Are you Catholic?"

"Mostly."

"I thought you told me you were something else."

"That was before Father Brannigan arrived."

Time to change the subject. "Let's get lunch. I'm about done with detective work for a bit." Bailey got into the passenger side and thought about next steps in the investigation, but all he could think about was dinner with Cara.

Across the lot, two people in a car watched them leave.

Down the street a lone man in an old truck watched the watchers.

CHAPTER 10

Luxury Penthouse Suite - Downtown Phoenix

The assistant city manager, mayor, the stocky man, and the tall, slender woman sat at a table before the man they knew as Carlo Bangor, the investor and political operative behind much of the state's elected class.

"Why is someone asking questions about the acquisition?" Bangor asked.

The mayor stuttered. "We don't know. It started with the Father Brannigan thing. It has to have something to do with the priest. Taking over that old church was the last piece of the puzzle."

"I want my data center to be the crown jewel of this project. To complete the project, I need all that space *and* the city's power plant. I put you where you are to make sure that I get everything I want, Mister Mayor. But if you screw this up, I stand to lose close to a billion dollars instantly and it only gets worse after that. So, understand me when I tell you I'm serious. And if I'm disappointed, there will be consequences."

The assistant city manager, an operative quietly put in place by Bangor spoke next. "The Mayor is letting a clown show happen right in his backyard." He looked at the mayor with disgust. "This fool can't keep his people in line. He's allowing the entire project to be put at risk."

The mayor shuddered in fear but said nothing. He

just hung his head like a whipped dog, knowing he was playing a life-and-death game he should have never gotten into in the first place.

The stocky man threw four eight-by-ten glossy surveillance photos on the table. "Who are these two? They were talking to the old priest today."

The mayor gasped. "That's Frank Bailey... and the black guy is a cop."

"Bangor asked impatiently, "Who in the hell is Frank Bailey?"

"He's like a madman. He's a retired lieutenant. He ran a team of renegade cops back in the eighties. Now he's back. He's on the citizens' police review board. I think he's working with Father Brannigan."

"You said that name before. Who the hell is this, Father Brannigan? Is he from the church building I want?" Bangor asked.

"No, much bigger. This guy is all over the news. A big shot Vatican investigator. Nobody knows why he's here. He came in with a team of commandos or something. It's awful."

"Are you mental?" Bangor asked.

The assistant city manager said, "No, he's right. It's been on the news. That famous newswoman, Cara Carter, she's covering it. Brannigan is supposedly. investigating the Mesa Police Department, or something to do with the city. It's vague."

"Cara Carter? With the..." He made a gesture of holding up big bosoms.

"Yeah, her. She's like the most well-known reporter in the Valley."

"Why hasn't someone reported this to me?" Bangor raged. He was visibly angered to the point of violence, which caused the mayor to start shaking like a constipated dog.

The thin woman said, "We only got these pictures today. We've picked up on this man. He has a group he's working with. They've been gathering at his residence. I'm not sure what they're up to. We also think he's working with the reporter."

Bangor started barking orders. "Have someone get rid of Bailey. He sounds like a problem. Bailey and the reporter both, and anyone working with them. If the priest doesn't sign off on the property transfer for the church, get rid of him to and have the city do an eminent domain to seize it. And if this Italian asshole Father Brannigan causes any problems, waste him too. I can't afford another week of dragging this out. It sounds like if Bailey is gone, our problems are gone."

The thin woman and husky man smiled. She said, "We can get Bailey tonight."

The husky man added, "The woman too."

The Compass Room

Bailey waited at the table, enjoying the view from the twenty-fourth floor as the restaurant slowly rotated, providing diners with a new view of the valley every few minutes. He sipped a sparkling water. Facing a drive across town later, he'd skip the alcohol for now.

As the clock struck eight, Cara Carter made her entrance. As a local TV celebrity, she drew a lot of attention. The outfit helped too. She wore a dark purple floor length gown with a long slit and a low-cut top revealing even a lot more cleavage than usual, which was an amazing feat in itself.

Bailey stood and greeted her. They did cheek kisses.

That's a start, he thought. Then he mentally cursed himself. *Who's kidding who? I'm seventy-one years old. She's having a mercy date with me and that's all.*

They sat down and Bailey asked her what she'd like to drink.

"I took a ride-share, so, I'll have a Don Camilo on rocks with a lime twist."

"Good taste."

The waiter arrived and Bailey ordered the tequila for Cara.

"So, how was the broadcast?" Bailey asked, not sure how to make small talk with a reporter.

"It went great. We interviewed a few more witnesses to the Father Brannigan miracle and I think I found some new corruption information at City Hall."

"Really? Intriguing. How so?"

"You show me yours and I'll show you mine."

"Oh, my pending story?"

"Yeah, you should *really* give it up," she raised her eyebrows once and said in a sexy whisper, making it ambiguous as to what exactly she wanted him to give up.

Her flirtatious words left Bailey feeling a bit awkward and uncomfortable. *There's no fool like an old fool;* he kept reminding himself. *She's only being silly. Nothing more.*

"Now that you mention it, I think you could help us, Cara. But I hate to talk business over dinner. What kind of host would I be?"

She didn't give up on her charm campaign, rather

she doubled down. "An experienced, distinguished, charming, rugged one. You know, the kind of host I like."

Bailey thought, *I'll be dead soon enough. Old fool or not, might as well go down swinging for the back fence.* "Are you really that hungry, or are you *really* that hungry?

She smiled a devilish grin, "My condo is ten minutes away."

Bailey couldn't believe that line worked, but why argue with success? "I'll drive."

He called the waiter over and paid for the drinks with cash. "Keep the change."

The elevator ride down could have gotten them arrested if anyone else had boarded the car. But they made it to the parking garage with their clothing intact. The couple walked hand-in-hand to the Mercedes. Bailey broke the first rule of good fortune and jinxed himself with a moment of vanity. *At this moment, I am the coolest guy on the planet.* Then Steve McQueen looked down from Cool Guy Valhalla and humbled him with an awkward and embarrassing trip over a crack in the concrete flooring.

The first shot just missed Bailey's right ear as he stumbled.

Bailey went with the stumble, and shoulder rolled forward behind a big pickup truck. He reached out to pull Cara to safety behind him, but she peeled off and dove behind the left-front wheel of a full-size Chevrolet. To his surprise she pulled a black automatic pistol out of... *somewhere* on her slinky dress and began engaging targets.

Bailey spotted two people near a Cadillac SUV. One with a long gun and the other with a pistol.

They both emptied magazines in his direction, pinning him down.

As the attackers focused on Bailey, Cara assumed a combat stance, the slit of her dress revealing a long leg and a thigh holster. Her hair was wild, and fire was in her eyes as she looked down the front sight of her weapon and mag-dumped the threat, then slipped behind cover and reloaded.

A pause.

Bailey held fired and listened. A grunt and a thud. He leaned around and fired three rounds.

Fast footsteps, a yelp and a curse, a car engine.

The pair of assassins was in retreat. In seconds, the Cadillac shot out of its parking space, engine roaring and tires squealing. The big SUV flew out of the parking facility exit and onto the street.

Cara yelled at the attackers as she reloaded. "Second Amendment, bitches!"

Where did she keep that spare magazine? Bailey wondered.

Cara yelled, "Are you okay, Bailey?"

Bailey yelled back, "I'm good. Are you okay?" he lied about being okay. He hadn't done a shoulder roll in thirty years and felt like maybe he might need two or three medics and a gurney. *I might have been better off letting them shoot me.*

Cara gave him a thumbs up. "Let's go."

In the name of male ego, Bailey sucked up the pain. They cleared the area tactically, confirming all the assailants abandoned their attack and left the area.

Bailey said, "We must have hit one of them." He

pointed to a small pool of blood near where the Cadillac was parked.

"Maybe both," she said, pointing out another blood trail further down and some broken glass from a car window. "Who in the hell was that?"

"I don't know, but I picked a hell of a time to give Jones the night off."

"Should we report it?"

Bailey considered the option of calling Phoenix PD for a moment and said, "No. I'd rather stay off book." He pointed at the exit the shooters escaped from. "They'll go lick their wounds and try to figure out how to explain to their boss that they fucked up the job. And I don't want to be stuck here all night with Phoenix PD explaining why we shot up a parking garage with no bad guys to show for it." He turned to her and smiled, "Let's get the hell out of here. I believe we had other plans."

Cara smiled back. "You're the boss."

Gunfights are the best aphrodisiac, he thought.

Ten minutes later, they were resuming their earlier elevator activities in her living room. And then later, her bedroom. Before he fell asleep, Bailey texted Jones: *Buffalo soldier, Unknown parties tried to kill me earlier in Phx. Stay on your toes and inform others. Baddies are on offense. I'll be back in AM. B.Moses.*

Cara asked him, "Who are you texting?

"A couple of hot chicks in case I wear you out."

She laughed and play slapped him. "You wish."

"I *do* wish. But they say wishes never come true."

She softly caressed his face with her hand. "Sometimes they do."

Luxury Penthouse Suite - Downtown Phoenix

Bangor wasn't simply furious, he was in a state of nearly uncontrollable rage. He snatched random items from his desktop and threw them at the man and woman standing before him as he screamed and swore. They dodged the missiles as best they could, standing stoically before his massive desk.

"How can you fools screw this up so badly? What the hell is wrong with you? Do I not pay you enough for competence?"

The man tried to explain again. "Sir, he stumbled as I pulled the trigger. It would have been a clean head shot."

"Center mass, you idiot. He was on a date. He wasn't wearing a vest. You should have put that round through his pitiful little heart. And now both of you are here making excuses, bleeding like pathetic dogs on my fifty-thousand-dollar Persian rug."

They both stepped back off the carpet.

Bangor whispered angrily, "It was supposed to look like a robbery. That's what you told me. You said this would look like a simple parking garage robbery. How in the hell could you fuck this up?"

They had no answer.

Bangor pushed recriminations aside and shifted to problem solving. "How badly are you hurt? Can you still work?"

The woman, knowing that the health plan for this job consisted of a bullet to the back of the head, answered. "I cut my hand on some broken glass, it's nothing. He was only grazed above the ear. We're fine."

Bangor instantly flipped back to recriminations and

another rant.

"Grazed above the ear," Bangor chided. "You missed a headshot with a rifle from a position of cover. But a has-been cop, who should be in a nursing home, popped you in the brain bucket with a fucking pistol. You people disgust me." Bangor spun away and turned his back to them, looking at the ceiling like an answer might be written up there.

The woman asked, "Sir, what do you want us to do?"

"What are we facing?

"Same as before. Father Brannigan and his team. Bailey, the reporter, the small group of cops we've seen running in and out of his apartment. Maybe four or five of them.

"Get more help and finish it. Tomorrow night. This time, no loose ends. Scorched earth. Take everyone down. We're too close to let this slip away. Did I mention a billion-dollar loss right off the bat if this goes south?"

"We only have four operators left we can trust with something like this."

"Then take them. Six of you better be able to take down a septuagenarian, a newsreader, and a few lousy third-string cops for what I'm paying. Now fix this and don't come back until you do. And it might be time to get rid of that idiot mayor. He knows too much now. And maybe that buffoon police chief too. He should have shut this thing down weeks ago. Move our assistant city manager into the mayor's position. Find me a police chief from San Francisco or Portland. Call the people who arrange that."

"Yes, sir. But what about Brannigan?"

"Do you know where he is?"

"No."

"Then deal with Bailey first. Then find Brannigan. Do I have to do this myself? Now get out of here. I need to think."

The pair turned and left. Bangor flopped into his chair and pouted. *I won't lose,* he thought. *Not this time, not ever.*

Bailey's Apartment

At eight in the morning, the team members shared copies of their investigative notes with each other as Bailey spoke.

"I called an emergency meeting this morning for everyone's safety. Parties unknown made a move on myself and Cara Carter last night in the parking garage of the Compass Room in Phoenix last night at about twenty-forty-five hours. There was a brief gunfight, and we might have hit one or both of them. Unfortunately, they escaped the scene. All of you are at risk."

Patch, Slay, Ma, Jones, and Gumby sat quietly as Bailey ran down the entire details of the incident. When he completed his briefing, Ma said, "So, you're saying you had a date with Cara Carter, the one with the boobs?"

"We just had dinner, Ma. That's all," Bailey lied poorly." *Note to self: never tell a blatant lie in front of a pack of experienced cops.* "But forget about that. We need to focus on this murder attempt. All of us are potential targets."

Slay didn't let it go. "Lieutenant, by definition, that *is* a date. How long has this been going on? When were you going to notify us that you were dating someone?"

Patch jumped in. "How are we supposed to protect you if you don't tell us about these things, Lieutenant. It's a cruel world out there. Women can be evil. Not that it isn't worth it. But still, I've singlehandedly paid off my divorce attorney's student loans and his kids' student loans. God willing, I'll live long enough pay off his grandchildren's student loans. There are consequences to love, sir. I'm living proof. You really need to run these things by us, Lieutenant."

Bailey attempted to deflect. "It was just dinner, and we only talked. She wanted to know about the citizen review board." *Why did I just say that? That was a shitty lie. I can lie better than this.* "Now, let's get back to the hit job..."

Ma interrupted, waiving a finger, "At the Compass Room? Dinner? Honey, you don't discuss the Citizen Review Board at the Compass Room with a set of knockers like that without running it by Ma first. I don't want to see you get hurt. She might be young enough to have kids. That means child support coming out of your social security checks, selling your car, living in a single-wide trailer in Apache Junction. Not a good look for you, sir."

Bailey objected, "Now wait! You guys are missing the point. Assassins are trying to kill us all."

Gumby weighed in, "I predicted this date. I venture to guess this relationship is far more serious than we imagined. Due to the serious nature of this subject matter, I think we will need to have the truth, sir."

"Did you morons miss the part about someone is trying to kill us? By us, I mean everyone in this room? Did you forget about the bum murders?"

Ma said, "Bum murders and assassins can wait. This is important. Now confess everything, or we'll question her. *Then* we'll decide what to do with this information."

Bailey gave up. "Fine. It was a date. I like her. And she

probably shot one of the suspects. She carries a Glock 26 in a thigh holster and she mag-dumped the bad guys to give me cover. So, there... I like her. Oh, and she hates the other reporters, she likes cops, and I think we ought to bring her in on the bum murders to run cover for us with the media. That's it. Are you happy now?"

Slay made a face like he just made the last payment on his car, "I'm satisfied."

Patch gave a thumbs up. "Me too."

Jones, who had been quiet, said despondently, "I should have been there."

Ma gave Jones a motherly pat on the knee. "It's going to be fine, Jones. Don't worry. I promise, we'll let you finish off each of these murdering dirtbags one by one in some horrible way." Then she gave Jones a little pinch on the cheek.

A somewhat comforted Jones replied, "Thank you, Ma."

Touching. Bailey wondered if Ma was going to pull out a hanky, have Jones blow his nose, and then tell him to go outside and play with the other cops.

Ma focused back on Bailey. "I'm happy now too, and I agree. We could use an outsider from the media to help with the City Hall blowback. And it sounds like she's trustworthy." She addressed the group. "Show of hands, who all thinks we should bring the Lieutenant's girlfriend onto the team?"

Bailey complained again, this time, whining like an eleven-year-old boy, "I don't have a girlfriend."

No one listened to him. The group vote was unanimous. Cara was in.

With the girlfriend business closed, Slay, went back to sorting through the investigative notes. He drove the conversation back to the business that placed their lives in jeopardy. "It looks like our next move is to find Meth Chick. We find her, secure her as our witness, identify the assassins, and then we nail the bad actors at City Hall."

Bailey replied, "We still have no clue as to who is financing all of this. Someone is writing big checks. That's the asshole we really want."

"And a *person or persons unknown* at City Hall is on the payroll of those fat checks," Patch said. "My inside source thinks there might be three City Hall workers and two big wigs. But they won't spill the details."

Bailey nodded. "I assume your source is a female, Patch. It's time to dial up the charm." He addressed the group. "You turds apparently have all this massive romance knowledge base, so let's put it to good use for a change rather than tormenting an old man. Work every angle and every snitch."

Patch couldn't tell if Bailey was trying to be humorous or if he was pissed off. He didn't want to risk being wrong, so he played it straight. "Yes, sir."

Gumby held up a hand. "I might have a few possible addresses for Meth Chick. It would be worth checking out tonight."

Bailey agreed. "Refine the list. Find the girl. Don't take any action though. We'll all meet here at seven this evening. I'll bring Cara and introduce her. She'll share what she has with us. She's been working public corruption for fifteen years. I think she will add some clarity that we don't see from working inside the city bubble. The rest of you work counter-surveillance.

They've been watching us. We need to watch them. Work as if it's a normal but, but if we get a chance, set a trap. Put the bag on them. I'll let you know where to take them if you get one. I have a place set up. Oh, and rule number one?"

"Don't get caught?" Ma asked.

"No, that *is* usually number one. But until we blow the lid off this thing, rule number one is don't get killed."

Jones said, "Then I need to stay on you, Lieutenant. I was supposed to protect you, and you almost got killed. You can imagine how embarrassing that would be if you were murdered."

Bailey smiled. "I agree, Jones. We can't have that." He thought for a moment. "But there are some things I don't want you to witness for the sake of your career."

"What do you want us to do if there is any shooting?"

"If there aren't any witnesses, and no bodies full of ballistic evidence, then your pals on the street and in dispatch should be clearing any calls on it as 'random gang violence, unknown suspects have left the scene.' Most of the time though, there aren't even any calls on that kind of thing. Citizens don't give a shit. So don't over think it. That's how we used to do it back in the old days."

Ma smiled warmly at the thought of shootings with no reports. "Nice."

"Gumby, if you find Meth Chick, call me. I'll handle it from there."

"Are you sure?"

"Yeah, I'll bring Cara as a backup. No police careers will be put in jeopardy that way. But I *will* get the information out of her tonight… the *old* way."

A chill fell over the room at Bailey's last three words. The others looked at each other with a mix of fear and joy. They weren't sure *exactly* what he meant by *the old way*, but they were reasonably certain it was going to be something very bad. According to ancient cop lore, the detectives from the eighties were capable of almost anything, even stuff the CIA wouldn't consider doing. If the rumors were true, and they were almost *always* true, Bailey was turning the clock back, all the way back to the era of the eighties renegade cops. A time of two-fisted detectives who don't play by the rules. Cops who are borderline outlaws themselves. Fighting bad guys on their own terms. Was the golden age of police work finally returning?

Patch looked longingly out the windows into the night sky. *If only we had a fat sweaty captain with his tie half undone screaming at us about the mayor being on his ass, then suspending us. If we still had captains. We should still have captains.*

Ma gazed out the same window. *I might not be the hot young recruit I started out as. And I might have given birth to a vague number of snotty rug rats since I got hired. And I might be a little over academy weight. But this is the shit I signed up for. Finally, being a real cop!*

Bailey closed out the meeting with a question. "Jones, can you get your hands on a big old hairy-assed fucking machine gun?"

"I'm not sure exactly what that means, but yes, sir. Yes, I can."

"Go get it."

"Yes, sir."

"And a bunch of ammo. I didn't care for being

outgunned last night."

"Yes, sir."

Patch elbowed Slay and whispered, "This is the greatest day of my life."

Bailey finished with words for all, as he made focused eye contact with each of them, one by one. "The rest of you, stay alive...The mission is simple. Draw out the perps." He paused for effect. "Then bag the perps by any means necessary."

The crew was wound up, barely able to remain seated. Their enthusiastic mutterings were kept low as they clung to every word.

Bailey wrapped his speech up with a dismissal. "Now, you clowns get the hell out of here. I've been up all night. It will be a long night tonight. And an old man needs to get some sleep." He turned and went back to his bedroom, concealing the grin on his face. *Best time ever.*

As they said their goodnights and filed out, Slay thought, *this is the greatest day of my life too.*

Apartment Complex - Southeast Mesa

Meth Chick peeked out the window, pulling the curtain back with her bony tattooed hand. *Is it the dope or is someone out there?* Hiding inside her ex-boyfriend's cousin's neighbor's abandoned apartment since scoring from Fanta seemed like a safe enough plan. But the drugs were running out. *Someone is following me. I know it. But who?*

She'd been up for three days straight, and the onset of sobriety was exhausting. *It's a bad time to crash. but maybe just a short nap on the couch.*

CHAPTER 11

City Hall

The Mayor paced in his office. Everything was falling apart. It all started with that lunatic Bailey. He called the police Chief on the Chief's private burner phone.

The chief's first words were, "We're not supposed to use these unless it's an emergency."

"This is an emergency. Bangor is pissed."

"Don't say his name."

"He's still pissed. You were supposed to put a lid on Bailey and now he shot one of you-know-who's guys. You got to get Bailey under control."

"But he's mean," the chief whined.

"I know," the Mayor whined back.

"So, what do we do?" The chief asked.

"We need a Plan B or this whole thing is going to blow up in our faces. You-know-who got us these jobs. He can get us fired, or worse, we could get indicted."

"Or worse than that, killed," the chief moaned.

"I know," the mayor whined again.

The chief echo-whined, "I know!"

The Mayor bleated woefully, "Right? I'm freaking out."

"Me too. Maybe we confront Bailey and get him to leave town. Or we can pay him off or something. There are millions to be made here. Maybe we can use some of that to bribe him," the chief suggested.

"He might try to citizen arrest us if we try that."

"We don't have a choice. I don't think you-know-who will help us."

The mayor's bladder ached. "Call me later. I have to pee." He disconnected and scurried to the door with his legs awkwardly held together as he darted for the bathroom. Fear made him pee, and he was as frightened as a fat camper running from a hungry grizzly bear.

The mayor's receptionist put the glass she used to listen through the door in a desk drawer. She waited for him to get down the hall before she called Patch.

"Sergeant Jim Patch."

"You know who this is."

"Hi beautiful."

"Hi. Hey, I got something for you."

"What's up?"

"The Mayor and the police chief are shitting their pants. They might try to bribe that Bailey guy. They have a bunch of money from something going on they're going to use. I don't know what it is yet."

"Perfect, baby. Let me know when you find more. I owe you."

"You know what I want for payment," she cooed.

"Behave! You work for the City. Show some decorum."

"I got some decorum to show you."

Patch laughed. "Thanks for the heads up. I'll call you tonight."

He disconnected and texted Bailey using the burner:

Mayor & Chief plan 2 bribe u. Big $ involved. Heads up.

Heavenly Saint Catholic Church

Father Garcia was alone, praying from a pew after his meager lunch of a warm tortilla and glass of water. *Someone must save my church. That is all I ask.*

The men came in, two of them. They entered through a back door. One carrying a baseball bat. One carrying an axe.

Father Garcia didn't notice them until it was too late. He felt the blow of the bat against his shoulder, sending him sliding down the pew, then onto the floor. The men were on top of him before he knew it.

"Sign off on the transfer or die, old man."

He looked up to see they were wearing ski masks. They tossed a folder and a pen down at him. The man with the axe held it high, standing on a pew, ready to strike a death blow. The priest closed his eyes, preparing for his imminent demise. He could never sign his church away to men such as these, even if it meant an axe to the head.

Then, his ears burst with holy thunder, leaving them ringing so painfully, he could barely hear.

The man holding the axe flew across the room like a bloody, red meteor, landing in a heap of bone and meat in front of the pulpit. Then, there was the unmistakable sound of a twelve-gauge shotgun racking another shell into the chamber.

Baseball bat man pissed himself. "Who the hell *are* you?"

Father Garcia peeked up to see a man standing on a pew in the back of the church, pointing a shotgun at the man with the bat. He was wearing some kind of black floppy hat, a black cape, and a black shirt. He wore a mask. Was this Zorro?

The man announced himself. "My name is Father Brannigan, Vatican, Italy. You have frightened my priest. And desecrated this church. Repent sinners."

Father Garcia was confused. He thought that sounded a lot like a line from that old movie with André the Giant, but it was the other guy who said it, but he remembered André said something about a peanut. Then he smelled something foul. The attacker should have worn his brown pants.

"Please! Don't kill me, Father Brannigan." Fear immobilized the attacker. The word on the street was that Father Brannigan, the harbinger of death and pain far worse than one could ever imagine, never took a prisoner alive. He just took heads. And his partner was living proof. Well, maybe not so much *living*.

Brannigan spoke in a basso profondo voice. "Then tell your boss to leave this church in peace. Tell him to get out of Mesa forever or I shall return and collect both of your souls."

With that the man with the bat turned and ran leaving a trail of body fluid in his wake. When Father Garcia looked again, Father Brannigan had disappeared into the ether.

Father Garcia sprinted to the alter to give thanks, stepping over various remains of the axe man. Then he called 9-1-1.

The Mayor's Office

The phone in the Mayor's office was blowing up. The receptionist was screening them as best she could and only forwarding department heads.

"Father Brannigan just killed a guy!"

It was the police chief in a state of panic.

"What are you going to do about it?" The mayor asked, hoping it didn't require his involvement. The wrath of this mysterious Vatican Vigilante was not something he wanted to deal with.

The chief had no good answers. "I don't know. Apparently, it was a clean shoot. As far as anyone knows, he saved a local priest from a robbery. All Brannigan did was leave the scene of a crime. But even that won't stick. Every Catholic in town thinks he performed another miracle. Even my Catholic police officers are down there paying respects, doing whatever it is they do. We have nothing, and Father Brannigan is in the wind. I tried to tell all of you he was real. And now he's killing us off, one by one!"

The mayor hung up. He had to pee. This was bad. *Where can I buy a gun?*

Outside the office, his receptionist dashed away from the door as she heard his footsteps heading out for the fifth bathroom run in the last hour since the news broke. As soon as he was gone, she made a call to Patch with a full update.

Bailey's Apartment

"That can't be possible," Bailey muttered, waking up after a solid five hours of sleep.

"Why?" Patch asked, as he relayed his latest update to the Lieutenant.

"No reason. It just is. I'll talk to you later. I got to call somebody." Bailey disconnected and dialed Cara.

Cara's voice was warm and welcoming. "Hey, Handsome."

Frank sounded desperate. "Cara, did you hear about the shooting?"

"Sure, everyone is talking about it. I think it just saved my job at the station. It proved I was right about the whole Vatican Investigation. I'm heading to the church now."

"Can you pick me and Jones up? We know the priest. Maybe we can help each other on this."

"Sure thing."

Jones came out of his room with a dumbbell in each hand. "Did you hear about Father Brannigan? He performed another miracle. He made an asshole disappear off the face of the earth..."

Bailey interrupted. "Yeah, that's just an initial report, Jones.

"...and he made another one shit his pants."

"Right. That's definitely feels like some kind of miracle, Jones. Suit up. We're heading over there. Cara is on the way over here. She's going with us."

Jones had seen Cara Carter on the television news for years. "The reporter? That might be a miracle too. Cops and reporters teaming up to fight evil. When this is over, I'm formally joining up. Maybe I'll even become a priest."

"Priests take a vow of abstinence."

"I'll probably just do a regular membership then. I'm not really ready for a priesthood gig."

"Right." Bailey's mind was racing. Is this a copycat? Who got blown away? Who do they work for? Are they coming for us next?

Half an hour later, Cara arrived at Bailey's door. "Nice digs." She gave Bailey a hug and a peck on the cheek.

"Thanks, Cara. This is Jones."

"Nice to meet you Jones."

Jones was starstruck. "I've seen *you* on television." He was paralyzed with awe at interacting with a television personality like a real person.

"Yes, I *am* on television. Makes perfect sense." She reached out and found his right hand, which was dangling limply at his side, and shook it. "I'm Cara. I'm looking forward to working with you."

Jones stood slack jawed and motionless, unable to speak.

Bailey said, "Don't worry about him. He'll be fine. What did you drive?"

"My SUV."

"We better take that. I don't think three of us will be comfortable in the Benz." He did a subtle nod towards Jones indicating the problems associated with transporting a man equal to a party of four.

"Sounds good. Let's go." She took the big cop by the hand, walking a zombified Jones out.

"Is your cameraman here?" Bailey asked.

"Yeah. He is in his own car. He wouldn't come up. He's afraid you'd shoot him or something."

"Smart kid."

Ten minutes later they were at the church. A police circus was still underway with a mobile command post, a media zone, and a lot of yellow tape. Jones was coming off his initial shock of seeing a television personality in the flesh and was becoming slightly more communicative.

Bailey said to him. "Go get Father Garcia and bring him around back where it isn't so crowded, if you can. We'll roll up and get him in the SUV. Otherwise, the cops might have a problem."

"We are the cops."

"I'm not."

"Oh yeah. I forgot."

A few minutes later they had Father Garcia in the back seat of the SUV, and they were rolling south towards a remote parking lot at a dead shopping mall. A safe place to talk.

Bailey started. "What did you see, Father?"

Cara was whispering something into the camera feed about a secret location and interview by a former lieutenant.

Father Garcia said, "I saw a miracle. I was about to die. I prayed for my church when all of the sudden out of nothing, Father Brannigan appeared. He was like a ghost."

"Can you describe him?"

"He was about nine feet tall. He floated in the air like a bird. He wore dark clothes, a long black cape, and a black floppy hat."

Jones interjected, "Like Batman?"

Father Garcia thought about that one a moment. "Yeah, but more like Keaton, not Affleck."

Great, another Holy Batman sighting. That really gives this credibility. But maybe that works in my favor. Bailey asked, "What, if anything, did he say?"

"He said, Hello, my name is Father Brannigan, you killed my father, prepare to die. Or something like that."

Priests must watch a lot of movies. "Then what?"

"He blasted that piece of caca right out of his socks with a gigantic machine gun." The priest reenacted the shooting. "Ka-Blam Blam Blam!" Then, looking embarrassed, he sat back down quietly.

"No kidding?" Bailey was impressed. The reenactment looked more like a scene out of Scarface. He noticed Jones doing signs of the cross out of the corner of his eye. *But something isn't adding up* "Then what?"

The priest leaned in, and stage whispered. "Then... Father Brannigan just vanished, again, like a ghost. It was a miracle. I never thought I would witness a true miracle, but on this day, I did."

Bailey couldn't process how any of this was remotely possible. He gave up. "Your witness, Cara." Bailey stepped aside for a cigarette while Cara delved into another line of questions with the old priest.

Something weird is going on here.

A marked unit rolled up. Supervisor was written on the fender. It was Slay. He got out of the car of and approached Bailey. "Please don't tell me you have the missing priest, Lieutenant."

"Okay, I won't tell you."

"Shit. They have everyone out looking for him. How did you get him out of there."

"Miracle. Haven't you heard? They're the latest thing. Happening everywhere."

"Come on, boss. It's the team's ass if the brass finds out you snatched him. Let me take him back. I'll tell them I found him out wandering around for some fresh air."

"Cool. Thanks, Slay. You still on for briefing tonight?'

"Definitely."

Bailey banged on the side of the SUV to get everyone's attention and announced it was time to go. They loaded the little priest into the marked unit and Slay whisked him back to the crime scene.

Bailey, Cara, and Jones got back inside the SUV. Bailey announced, "I should go home. I need to get ready for tonight."

Cara agreed. "I have to go to the station and get my story in the can. Afterwards, I'll meet you guys for briefing. If we break this story, I'm retiring and running for congress. I want to go out on a blockbuster."

Bailey cautioned, "Let's not get ahead of ourselves. Can Jones stay with you as a bodyguard? I'm not leaving the apartment, so I'll be okay."

"Sure, if it's okay with Jones. I'd love the company."

Jones grinned, which seemed to strain his face muscles. "Hell yes! This is my first celebrity bodyguard gig."

Cara surreptitiously winked at Bailey. "Don't worry. I won't let anything happen to him."

Bailey winked back. "I'll see you all tonight then. Drop me off at home on the way."

Central Mesa

The ancient little two-bedroom house with detached garage worked perfectly for a command post. Using a fake identification and working with a shady realtor, he was easily able to score the place for a couple of months with hard cash.

The garage was surrounded by dense shrubs and trees, the alley rarely used. It was perfect for his work. The man busied himself melting down the components of the shotgun with the welder he picked up at a thrift store and tossing his clothes and rubber gloves into a bin to burn and then bleach the ashes.

He went to the corner of the garage and used another bucket of soap and water that he poured over himself before a thorough scrub and a rinse. Then he pulled on some sweatpants and a jersey and went into the house to get prepare for the next miracle.

They didn't think I'd come back, he thought. Then he smiled. Mayor Henry should never have resurrected me.

Luxury Penthouse Suite - Downtown Phoenix

"Can that body in the church be tied to me?" Bangor asked, visibly angered.

"Not possible. He never met anyone but her and I. He had no idea who we were working for." The stocky man explained.

"And so, Father Brannigan is real after all."

"Apparently. We didn't think it was possible. But he was there. Our man talked to him."

"And what did he say?"

"He said Brannigan told him to get out of town and leave the church alone, more or less. The guy was pretty freaked out. He said this Brannigan guy is a giant, dressed in some kind of black cape and mask, and he had some kind of huge machine gun like Rambo. It was crazy."

"Are you sure?"

"Well, he was pretty freaked out, but he seemed sure."

"Why did I not know about this? I own a mayor, an assistant city manager, a police chief. And I have you two placed in City Hall to keep them in line. And this Brannigan thing seems like total bullshit. How can a demon hunting priest from Italy investigating evil in Mesa be a real thing?"

"Well, it was on television, sir," the stocky man said.

Bangor lost it. He came around from his desk and screamed in muscle head's face. "Television is bullshit, you idiot. Grow up!" He turned, suddenly calm, and asked the tall, thin woman, "Do we have any men left?"

"The guy who shit his pants, two other guys, and us."

"Then get rid of these cop vigilantes, the priest vigilante, the little priest, any witnesses, and end this thing, this time for sure... and get rid of that dumb ass mayor first. He's a little pussy and he knows too much. He'll talk. Make it look like Brannigan did it."

"Yes, sir."

"If we don't get control of this in the next seventy-two hours, I'm folding this operation and heading for Pacific Palisades. There are real estate opportunities there right now, maybe better than this."

"Yes, sir," the pair said like soldiers in a formation.

"Get out there and fix it, because you won't like what happens if you don't."

Oscar's Gun Emporium, Mesa, Arizona

The sign out front said: Oscar's Gun Emporium - The Only Good Communist is a Dead One.

Probably not one of my voters. The mayor parked his city vehicle on a side street in the back and walked around the block. He didn't want anyone else to know he was escalating his personal defense options.

He got to the entrance and stopped. *I can't go through with this.* Then he thought about the man who put him in office and what he does to those who don't deliver the goods as told.

The hell with it. I'm packing heat. He felt a little better imagining himself being tough.

The mayor knew nothing about guns except he needed one. *How hard can it be? I watch TV. Shooting looks easy.* He was in deep over his head with a pack of dangerous criminals controlling his every move and a vigilante priest who was killing everybody involved in the scam. The time for self-preservation had arrived.

A bell on the door jingled as he entered the store. He could see two men working on guns in a back room through an open doorway behind the counter. One of them came out, a tall, husky man with a bushy beard, jeans, suspenders, a big scary gun on his hip, and a ball cap. He looked like a gun owner. Big, tough, violent, mean, conservative, he could fix his own truck... every trait the Mayor hated in his own gender.

The man said pleasantly, "How can I help you today, sir."

"I need a gun for self-protection."

"Do you know what kind of gun you prefer?"

"A cop gun."

The man looked as concerned as a doctor forced to write a heroin prescription for a junkie. He *was* in the business of selling guns, but he hated selling guns to stupid people. "May I ask if you ever had any training, sir."

The mayor lied. "Of course I have training. I took the RNA course."

"Do you mean an NRA course?"

"Whatever. Just sell me a cop gun and I'll be out of

here." He tossed his ID on the counter and arrogantly peeled out five crisp one-hundred-dollar bills from his wallet.

The man looked at the money, then suggested politely, "Sir, if I could suggest, you might want to go visit a range, spend some time with various weapons, and perhaps work with a trainer before you commit to buying a firearm.

The mayor lost his patience, his hubris getting the best of him. *No two-bit local small business owner talks to me like that,* he thought. He put the gun salesman on blast. "I don't have a lot of time to waste. I want a gun. You have guns. Sell me a gun. Or are you too stupid to understand a simple business transaction?"

The store owner sized up the man and decided to give him the premier customer service he reserved especially for this type of consumer. "Fine. The customer is always right, sir. Let me see what we have." He dug around the back of the display case. "This... is a cop gun." He surreptitiously pulled the price tag off a cheap, well-used ninety-five-dollar knock-off-brand automatic and placed the gun on the counter. "This weapon typically sells for fifteen-hundred dollars. It's on sale today only for five-hundred cash. I'll even toss in a box of ammo."

"I'll need a holster," the mayor said brusquely, bringing his highly honed negotiating skills into play.

"No problem, sir." The man put a box of nine-millimeter re-loaded practice rounds and a well-used five-dollar nylon holster on the counter. "You drive a hard bargain, but it *is* the end of the month, so you got me over a barrel."

The other worker in the back room looked at the

calendar. *It's the fifteenth.*

"Will you need a receipt?" The salesman asked.

"No."

"There is a form you're required by the Feds to fill out."

"Give it to me."

The man helped him fill out the required form and did the required background check. Taking advantage of an idiot was one thing. Screwing with the law was something else. As soon as the background check cleared, he turned and smiled. "Okay, you're good to go, sir. Happy hunting."

"Thanks." The mayor paused, looked about the store awkwardly, and then quietly asked. "Can you, uh... put the bullets in the thing, and the thing in the gun. And the gun in that nylon thing? Then I'll be all set."

"Whatever you need, Wyatt Earp."

The counterman quickly set up the cheap pistol rig and jacked a round into the chamber. "Just so you understand, sir, if you pull the trigger, this weapon will now go bang. Do *not* remove this weapon from the holster while you are in the store. If you do, we *will* shoot you. We will shoot you a lot."

"Fine." The mayor looped it onto his belt under his sport coat. He felt safer already.

The salesman lied a pleasantry, "Thank you for shopping with us and please come back real soon."

The mayor ignored him, pushed back the ammunition box, and said, "You can keep these extra bullets. If I need more, I'll come back and buy them."

"Smart tactical move. There's nothing worse than a bunch of extra bullets. That's what we always say in the gun industry."

The other employee, who was still cleaning guns in the back, overheard his partner's response and shook his head. *I'm pretty sure we don't always say that in the gun industry.*

Nightfall on the Streets of Mesa

So far, no luck. Meth Chick was still in the wind. Gumby flipped on the headlights as he continued the search. Darkness falls upon the city early this time of year. He liked the darkness; it gave him an advantage. He glanced at his wristwatch. There was still an hour before the briefing, so he had time to sit on his final location for a while.

Gumby pulled into a convenience store parking lot and checked the address in his notebook. One last place to scout for Meth Chick. He put his notebook away and headed to the final dump on his list of dumps she might be hiding in. It was less than five minutes away. He rolled the window down on the black Escalade, a car he traded with one of the narcs for the night and let some cool night air in before this last reconnaissance. He needed new cover, and the big SUV was a good surveillance platform. Also, in the event he wound up with Jones in the car later, he'd need all the space he could get. The night air felt refreshing. The interior gets stuffy real fast sitting stationary with the windows rolled up and the engine off. Rolling down one of the heavily tinted windows while parked would cost him his quiet and invisibility advantage. Stoicism is an important characteristic for those who hunt people. Hours of breathing stale air and smelling your own body stench is part of the job.

The detective found a good surveillance spot and

parked. The street was pitch dark, lined with big, leafy trees, and no streetlights close to him. The sidewalk and surroundings were shadows and blackness. He hopped across the console into the passenger seat.

The target house was dark except for a dim light from the front room. All the blinds were drawn. There was no observable movement from within the residence. *That could mean she is unconscious, dead, not there, or was beamed aboard an alien spaceship to be probed in creepy ways. Never eliminate any possibility.*

Gumby retrieved his home-made thermal scanner from the back of the SUV. He gave the place a look through the lens. *At this range, it's difficult to say, but she might be sleeping in the front room.*

He waited. It's what special investigations cops do. They wait.

Twenty minutes later, he saw the blinds bend and a face peek out.

He made the call.

CHAPTER 12

Bailey's Apartment

Bailey and Cara relaxed on the balcony, waiting for the team to arrive, when the call came in from Gumby.

"I have an eye on Meth Chick."

"Send me the address." Bailey looked at his watch. He sent a group text to the team to delay the briefing for two hours. He snatched up a couple of things from around the apartment, stuffed them in his coat, and wrote Jones a note for when he returned from the gym.

He looked at Cara, focused and ready. "Let's go."

Fifteen minutes later, Bailey killed his headlights, rolling up quietly behind Gumby's SUV.

Gumby slipped out of his ride, came back to Bailey's car, and hopped into the back seat. "She's in there. I think she's alone. Probably watching TV in the front room." He looked suspiciously at Cara. "I venture to guess this is the girlfriend who is the television star?"

Cara smiled coyly. "Did I get a promotion?"

Bailey didn't let Gumby's prognostication derail his focus. "Gumby, Cara. Cara, Gumby. Get something to eat and then head back to my place. I moved the briefing back two hours, but Jones should be there. I'll take care of this."

"Are you sure you don't want cover, Lieutenant?"

"I got it handled. None of you guys need to lose your

job over what I do next. See you in an hour or so."

"Copy that."

"...and Gumby."

"Yeah?"

Bailey reached around and retrieved a microfiber cloth and a couple of heavy binder clips from the back floorboard. "Cover my license plate before you go, will you?

Gumby smiled. "No problem.

Gumby carefully covered the plate, got back into his Cadillac SUV, and left the area.

Cara asked with a bit of concern, "So, *what* are you going to do?"

"Take her to my interrogation space and ask her about the bum murders. Nothing serious. She's just a witness."

"Oh. Okay. What do you want *me* to do?"

"Shoot anybody who gives us any shit."

Cara's eyes widened. "What? Really?"

Bailey chuckled. "No, just document what she says. I'm not as good at remembering details as I used to be."

"No problem."

Bailey added, "But if anyone gives us any shit, shoot 'em."

He hit the gas, spun the Mercedes in the street, tires squealing, and then hit reverse, burning rubber, backing the car up through the yard to the front door. He hit a button and popped the trunk.

Cara gasped, "What in the hell are you doing?"

"Police work."

Bailey got out, pulled his automatic, and marched to

the door. "Police!"

He waited less than half a second before he kicked the door off the hinges.

Meth Chick screamed and ran in circles in the front room like a drug-addicted lunatic. He identified her instantly as the girl in the surveillance photo from Fanta's place. Bailey grabbed her by her hair, threw her on the floor facedown, pulled zip ties from the pillowcase he took from his console and secured her wrists and ankles. Then he pulled the pillowcase over her head, carried her out, tossed her into the trunk of his car, slammed the trunk shut, and peeled out like he was leaving the scene of a bank robbery with the FBI in pursuit.

Meth Chick screamed in the trunk.

Cara screamed in the passenger seat.

Bailey lit a cigarette as he wheeled over the sidewalk and out of the neighborhood over to the industrial park where his secret warehouse space was located.

When they arrived, he got out, opened the big overhead door, pulled the car in, and closed the door behind him. There were three chairs and a chainsaw in the room. The place was only illuminated by the car headlights.

Bailey got Meth Chick out of the trunk and sat her in a chair. He took another chair. Cara sat in the car, unsure if any of this really just happened.

Meth Chick was shaking. "You're going to kill me this time, aren't you?"

Bailey kept his voice low. "I'm not those same people."

"Oh, thank goodness."

"I'm worse."

"Shit."

"Tell me about the people who took you last time."

"Aren't they your partners?"

"Tell me about the people who took you last time. I won't ask again. Although I should tell you there is a chainsaw in the room. Just thought you'd like to know."

"Shit."

"What did they look like?"

She described the husky man and the tall, thin woman. She described their clothes: business style attire, black, tailored. She noticed her shoes, black Chanel loafers.

Interesting observation, Bailey thought.

"How do you know the shoes?" Bailey asked.

"I used to work with a booster crew, shoplifting at Fashion Square in Scottsdale. We had to know the high-end stuff. You learn the fake from the real after a while."

"What happened to you?"

"Wait... didn't you yell *police* when you kicked the door in?"

"Yeah."

"So, you're a cop?"

"Not exactly."

"Are you even allowed to do this?"

"Only because it's a matter of national security. I'm working with Father Brannigan. You've heard of him."

"Yeah. He killed a guy in the Catholic Church down the street from where I was staying for disrespecting a priest. And he saved a baby, too."

"That's right. This is a joint CIA, Police, Vatican

operation, so technically, if you lie, we can send you to Gitmo."

Meth Chick nodded. "That makes sense."

Bailey thought, *No it doesn't. That's one of my worst lies ever. Do better, Bailey.*

Cara stayed in the car with the windows down, listening, between eye rolls and scribbling down every word in her notebook.

"So, what happened?"

"I was working the street. These two rolled up on me. Tried to get me in the car. Clipped me on the forehead with this big-assed hammer and did the trunk thing, like you. But I wasn't all the way out. I could still hear them talking."

"What did they say?"

"Something about Igor. And taking over some dating center. They work for the mayor, I think. I don't know. They said something about working at City Hall. Anyway, I just played dead. Then they took me to some place and was going to kill me, but I waited for my chance and then I fought 'em. They had on those white plastic suits they wear in the movies when some bad germ is destroying the world, so they couldn't fight real good. I surprised them, got out, and been on the run ever since."

Bailey went back to the car and asked Cara a question. "Do you have any photos of the mayor with his staff?"

"Sure, tons of them in my computer. I have quite a few in my phone, too, that I can access. Hold on."

She searched through her phone while Bailey made a quick call. "Jones, when everyone gets there, be ready. I'm sending you all some pictures in a few minutes."

Cara found a folder full of photos from recent events. Some had the mayor with his handlers, a tall, thin woman, and a shorter, stocky man. He picked the clearest one depicting the pair. Bailey took the phone back to Meth Chick and held it under the pillowcase. "Do you recognize anyone?"

"Yeah, those two assholes are the ones who kidnapped me."

He returned to the car and gave Cara her phone. "Send this photo to me, please." He showed her the photo Meth Chick identified. "These two kidnapped Meth Chick *and* they're the same assholes who tried to kill us at the garage. They're the mayor's handlers."

"Shit!"

"Yeah."

"So, what do we do with her? You kidnapped her, too. We're felons, Bailey."

"No, we're not. We're good guys. We can't be felons. This is what we call exigent circumstances."

"What?"

"It's an emergency situation that requires an unusual response. Totally routine. Don't worry about it."

Cara gave up. "Whatever you say. I'll just tell 'em I'm a hostage when we get arrested."

"Yeah, that works too."

He returned to Meth Chick. "Listen. You are a critical witness in a political corruption case. If I take you to jail, you might get murdered. If I release you in Mesa, you might get murdered. So, I'm going to give you three hundred bucks and drop you off in front of the fire station. I'll call a ride-share for you. It will take you to

Buckeye. Don't come back here for two days. But you *will* have to come back in two days, or you'll probably get murdered. I won't always be around to protect you if you don't do exactly as I say."

"You call this protection?"

"Yeah, are you dead?"

"No."

"You're welcome. Do you have an ID that's legit?"

"In my jeans pocket."

Bailey retrieved the ID, took a photo of it, and stuffed it back in her pocket. "So, are we good?"

"Yeah, we're good. I'm just glad I could help out Father Brannigan. I'm Catholic."

"Then get thee to a nunnery."

"Huh?"

"It's Shakespeare. It means be a nun or something like that. Or, it can mean, nice work. I'm sure Father Brannigan will be proud of you for helping. Either way, maybe you can start over after this. After all, you were almost murdered by serial killers and lived. That has to be some kind of sign."

"Nah, I'm good with my career. I'm starting an Only Fans and investing in Bitcoin. I've been studying digital currency."

Bailey shrugged. "Bitcoin. They say it's the future. Well, I have to respect an entrepreneur. Capitalism is what built this country. Good luck with it.

"Thanks."

"I'll reach out to you when we close the case and arrest these guys."

"Cool."

This time, he placed her in the backseat for the drive to the fire station. When they arrived, he called her a rideshare, helped her out of the car, then cut the zip ties with his knife. "You can pull the pillowcase off after you hear the car moving down the street. Are we good?"

"Yes, sir. Thanks for the ride and the cash. Good luck on the case."

"No problem. It was nice meeting you."

"It was nice meeting you, too, Father Brannigan."

Her words surprised Bailey. "What? No... I'm not him."

Yeah, right. I know who you really are. I knew it the minute you quoted Shakespeare. Only a cop who was a secret agent from the Vatican would say something like that. I'll always treasure this moment, Father."

Bailey decided this was one of those moments where if you can't beat 'em, join 'em. He gave her his Italian accent. "Bless-a you, my daughter. Please keep-a our little secret."

"I will, Father."

As they drove off, Cara asked, "Is that the way you used to interview witnesses back in the old days?"

"No, not all of them. Just the rude ones. Say, did you know it's not legally waterboarding if you use diesel?"

Cara gasped. "That's... horrifying. You can't really believe that." She paused. "Frank Bailey, what kind of man are you?"

"An effective one, I hope."

Luxury Penthouse Suite - Downtown Phoenix

Bangor made a call to the Mayor. "I want you in your office tonight. The advisors I provided you have information on Father Brannigan that you will need for a press conference tomorrow morning. Be there in two hours."

"I can't," the Mayor protested. "I have a council meeting and then dinner plans." He nervously touched the grip of his new gun.

"Be there after the council meeting. This is more important than your plans."

Bangor hung up and called the tall, thin woman. "I have him on his way to his office in two hours. Get rid of him *and* the Chief of Police. Blame it on Brannigan or the Chief or murder-suicide, I don't care. Just get rid of those two idiots. Then get rid of Bailey and those stupid cops. Take everybody we have with you in case there is a problem, as we discussed."

His calls finished, he got up from his desk and poured himself a drink. "I have to think of everything."

Bailey's Apartment

The crew was assembled, anxiously awaiting Bailey's return. Jones, as a temporary resident of the apartment, took command. "The lieutenant wants everybody ready to roll. I'm not sure what we're doing, but I think tonight is it."

"Do we have enough to make a bust?" Slay asked.

Jones deferred. "I'll let the lieutenant decide that."

At that moment, Bailey and Cara entered. There was the standard hush that goes with the arrival of a beautiful woman who is a combination stranger and celebrity into a closed social group.

Then Ma addressed her. "Welcome aboard, Cara. I'm glad you decided to join the good guys."

Cara was cautious. "I'm glad to be here. I hope we're the good guys. It's been strange so far." She looked around the room. The crew had maps, stacks of reports, photos, and equipment piled up. It looked like central command for a war. She thought, *in for a penny, in for a pound*, and added. "What do you say we kick some dirtbag ass?"

Her words broke the ice, and the group welcomed her with hugs and handshakes. But as the greetings subsided, they quickly got down to business.

Patch asked, "What happened?"

Bailey ignored the unpleasant details and got to the point. "We now know who the two main hitters are and that they work for the Mayor. And the Mayor works for someone named Igor, or something that sounds like Igor. We're almost ready to pop this thing."

That announcement led to some muted cheers and back slapping.

Ma Donna asked the million-dollar question. "How do we prove it?"

Bailey threw out thought bombs. "We either need the Mayor or one of the goons to talk. Or we need to find the paper trail that proves what they are up to. I know there is a motive to wipe out the city core, but what is it? My instincts tell me it's a land grab, but I don't know why. The core of the city, without an adjacent freeway exit, is done. There's too much blight to drive through from any direction to make it a destination. So, it's not valuable for resorts or business centers. There has to be something."

Cara raised her hand, unsure of how cop brainstorming sessions worked.

Bailey said, "Go ahead, the floor is open."

"Do you know the biggest issue in all the towns around here?"

Although her question was rhetorical, the team threw out rapid-fire guesses like cheerleaders shooting a t-shirt gun into a sport event crowd. "Assholes? Snowbirds? Traffic? Vegans? Canadians Commies? Heat? Californians?"

Cara was a bit overwhelmed by the enthusiasm. Cops were far more team spirited than reporters. "No, uh..."

Jones didn't quit. He felt like he was on to something. "It *is* Californians isn't it."

Cara put her hand up like an auctioneer closing the bidding. "No, it's power. Electrical power." She focused their attention on the bum murder map that Jones had taped to the wall earlier. "I did a story on this topic last month. The data centers are coming in and sucking up all the electrical power in the valley. They've been taking over big chunks of land in the outskirts of the metro-area. But they need more centers in the greater Phoenix core. The footprint of this murder map looks a lot like the gross area required for a medium-to-large sized data center. And the Catholic Church is right smack in the middle of it."

Slay asked, "Why would they want it here? Couldn't they just put it in Phoenix? Buy some warehouses?"

"Because of this." She pointed at the city power plant. "This is the only town that owns a power company. It can provide cheap power to the downtown area. They've done this for decades. I heard rumors that there was a move to rezone a lot of downtown and sell the plant, but the people pushed back. It goes against local identity, I guess."

Jones said, "We got some quirky identity shit in

this city, Cara. But they do love them some downtown Mayberry around here."

Cara continued, "I think they might want the power plant and the land. By they, I mean some hedge-fund manager or big investor. Someone powerful enough to install a mayor, put in a weak police chief, and place gangsters in City Hall."

Bailey mumbled, "C.K would have crushed these punks like a bug."

Cara asked, "Who?"

"Never mind. It was a long time ago. But I think you're onto something." He addressed the group. "We need to confront the suspects we have and get a confession out of them. Ma, can your accountant pal do some forensic work for us? Maybe figure out what's going on through public records and get us a name?"

"I'll ask."

"Slay, any idea where the Mayor is this evening?"

"They have a council meeting until about eight-thirty, then he will go out to eat or to his office. I don't know which he'll do first. But that's the usual routine with him."

"You and Patch keep an eye on him until Cara and I can get there with her cameraman to confront him on film. I think if we scare the shit out of him with what we know, he'll spill."

"Got it."

"And remember, there are still those two hitters out there looking for us. I suspect they know us all by now, so stay alert. No sense getting shot in the back."

"Copy that."

"Ma, when you're done with the accountant, meet us

at City Hall."

"Will do."

"Gumby, show the pictures of Tall Chick and Short Muscle Guy to Father Garcia. See if he's seen them around."

"Okay."

"Then I want you to work with the camera dude. He'll meet us in about an hour or so. He's kind of a pussy. We will need to capture some covert video tonight of whatever goes down with these nimrods. Either shoot it yourself or teach him how to be spooky."

"I can do that."

"Oh, and don't let them shoot him if things get hairy... that's totally optional."

"Can do." He scribbled the orders into his notebook.

"And Gumby."

"Yeah." Gumby looked up from his writing.

"Any predictions before we roll?"

The entire crew dropped what they were doing and stopped to listen to the forthcoming prognostication.

Gumby closed his leather notebook, carefully slipped it into his hip pocket, stood, and with one finger, pushed his glasses up to the bridge of his nose. "I predict..." He walked out onto the balcony and scanned the city for a long moment, then turned around and came back in. "I predict the city will fall."

An unusually cold breeze blew in from the open balcony windows adding to the spooky chill in the room at Gumby's words.

No one responded, they simply looked at each other, a

combination of fear, confusion, and awe filling their eyes.

There was an uncomfortable pause in the work.

Then slowly, quietly, the team resumed packing their gear and left on their missions. Jones went out to load his car and wait on the lieutenant and the reporter.

Only Bailey and Cara remained.

Bailey asked her, "Do you know what the heebie-jeebies are?"

"That?" as she stared blankly, pointing at the spot where Gumby made his dark prediction.

"Yeah, that."

City Hall

Patch and Slay took separate vehicles to cover the Council meeting. Patch remained outside on the street, ready to go mobile if the Mayor went out to eat afterwards. Slay went inside to call the surveillance or *take the eye* on the target. He would give the word on the any movement and interactions he observed.

The Catholic Church

Gumby went to the Church, but the priest wasn't there, which was odd. He was always there. But there were no signs of trouble. Gumby envisioned the trouble would be at City Hall. He'd check on the priest again later.

He went back to the apartment to wait for the cameraman. The time had come to wrap this case up.

City Hall

The tall, thin woman and stocky man led her team into the service entrance of the City Hall. In business attire, they blended into the evening activity.

The tall, thin woman gave her orders. "One of you wait

here at the door. When we give the word, be prepared to provide us cover if necessary, or have the car ready to go if we are not being followed. I'll let you know which."

The man who was the only human besides Father Garcia to be a confirmed eyewitness to Father Brannigan, volunteered for the job of guarding the door.

She continued, "I need to plant a suicide letter in the Mayor's desk. The rest of you be ready to snatch him when he returns from the council meeting and bring him to the roof. Then we hunt down the police chief. We've arranged for him to be here too."

The short, stocky man said, "I'll make sure we have the Mayor."

The group split up to carry out their assignments.

Downtown Brewery

Ma met with the accountant at a local downtown brewery. Over a draft, Ma presented what the team put together.

The accountant took it all in. "It makes perfect sense now. This explains everything from the residential real estate price drop, the Church move, the power plant. I know there was back-channel chatter going on again downtown about selling the power plant. I think you cracked it."

Ma said to her, "I think we're close, but we don't have hard evidence."

The accountant frowned. "You should bring in the FBI. I don't think the risk of telling the wrong person at City Hall or the Police Administration this information is worth it. Or maybe take it to that Father Brannigan guy. He's all people talk about. A one-man gangbuster squad and an outsider."

Ma said, "As far as I can tell, Brannigan works alone. Don't worry. When we get hard evidence, we'll make it public. Then the Bureau will have no choice but to jump in. We'll be protected that way."

"Good luck. This could get dangerous."

"It's already dangerous." Ma finished her draft, thanked her friend, and headed to City Hall.

City Hall

Slay put out a group text on the burners. *Meeting over. Mayor coming out front.* He casually walked out the side exit and headed for his car. Patch picked up the eye on the target.

***

The Mayor walked outside for privacy and phoned the Police Chief. "Get your ass up to my office now. Everything is turning to shit. I'll meet you there."

"This is your problem, not mine," the Chief complained.

"It's your problem too. If I go down, you go down, pal. Now get over here." The Mayor was feeling particularly tough now that he had a pistol. He imagined himself being a gunslinger in the old days. *I wish I knew how to twirl this thing.*

The Chief relented. "Fine, I'll be there in five."

***

Patch put out a group text of the play-by-play: *Mayor acting weird. Making a call outside. He's nervous. Not positive, but I'm pretty certain he's strapped. Now he's going back inside.*

Staying as far back as possible, Slay and Patch followed

the Mayor back into City Hall.

***

In the sub-basement of City Hall, a lone figure donned a black cape fashioned from a bolt of fabric and a shoestring, a long white wig, night vision goggles, and a large floppy hat. He cut the power to the building. An emergency generator provided dim red lights throughout the structure. He looked down at the man he met at the Catholic Church. "They're going to be pissed off when they find out you're down here instead of guarding the door, my son," he said as he stuffed two old Charter Arms Bulldog .44 Special revolvers into his waistband.

The man's voice was muffled under the canvas gym bag over his head, "Please don't kill me, Father Brannigan. I'll repent! I'll turn state's evidence! I'll do whatever you want!"

"Of course you will my son. But you will do these things for Bailey, not me."

"Who?"

"Commissioner Lieutenant Detective Frank Bailey. Remember that name," he said dramatically.

"I can't remember all that," the man whined.

The pathetic response broke the figure's focus on his dramatic flair. "Oh, well, uh... how much *can* you remember?"

"Maybe just the name, I think."

"Then, remember *Bailey*. Can you remember that much?"

"Yeah. Bailey. Like what you put in coffee...But you promise you won't kill me if I tell *him* everything, right?"

"Correct."

The man in the cape thought, *this is awkward. I feel like we had smarter hoods in my day. I should have stayed in Pittsburgh.* Then he reached under the bag and stuffed an old shop rag in the man's mouth

Outside City Hall

Bailey looked at the text message. *Strapped? The mayor with a gun? Why? A big complication.*

Bailey, Cara, Jones, Gumby, Ma, and the cameraman huddled outside Bailey's car. Bailey gave them the plan. "You guys saw Patch's message. The Mayor might be packing heat. That amps up the danger of a confrontation about a million percent."

Jones asked, "So what do we do?"

"We go ahead as planned. Cara and I are going to go in and confront the Mayor on camera. If he knows he's on camera, he probably won't pull a gun...but who knows, that goofy bastard might, but maybe not." Bailey hated this much uncertainty with Cara and Camera Guy around.

Gumby asked, "What about us?"

"The building should be empty. Maybe a janitor or two. I don't want him to see anybody but me and Cara. The rest of you just hide and listen. Gumby, you and Camera Guy try to stay invisible until the last minute. Can you do that?"

"No problem."

"It's now or never. There's no backing out now. We're all in, right?"

The team nodded and mumbled in agreement.

Bailey continued. "Ma, do you have the reinforcements in place?"

"Yeah, I have them at police headquarters waiting for a call."

"Get them staged with you out here." Bailey said, "Jones, I need you to make sure we don't have any surprises. Take the machine gun. Wrap it up in an overcoat or something. Gumby, as soon as we're done with the Mayor, I want you to search the place in stealth mode, find a place to watch for the chief. I have a feeling he's going to show up in the building somewhere. Let us know where he is and where he goes."

"What about witnesses?" Gumby asked.

"There shouldn't be anyone in the building except the one security guy. He won't do anything for a couple of hours. As soon as that council meeting ended, almost everyone started leaving. The security guy in the lobby will lock up the main floor soon. We go in through the side door."

"Do you have a key?" Ma asked.

"Mayor Henry gave me his keys before he left. A parting gift. It's almost like he *knew* this night would come."

Gumby said, "He's not the only one."

"What?"

"Nothing."

Bailey's burner phone received a call. It was Slay. "The power just went out in the building. Something weird is going down. I feel it."

"We're on the way. Stay with the Mayor."

"We lost sight of him already. But I think he got off the elevator on the top floor. He probably went to the office. We're taking the stairs."

"Copy that."

Bailey addressed the team. "It's turning to crap already. Let's go!"

Inside City Hall

The tall, thin woman placed the carefully crafted letter with the mayor's fingerprints and signature in the lap drawer of his desk, leaving the drawer slightly open. Tricking him into writing his name on a blank piece of paper was simple. Telling him the City Badging Office needed a sample for printing identification cards was all it took. Then typing the words, *It was all my idea, and I can't live with it anymore,* above the signature with an old city typewriter from the surplus and recycle equipment warehouse sealed the deal. No one would suspect anything nefarious from the suicide of this weak and unpopular mayor who Bangor installed in office with discrete election meddling.

Then, the building fell to total darkness, and a moment later, shifted an eerie glowing red. *Power failure.*

She suspected it wasn't accidental. Something else was going on. She pulled the Glock 17 from the shoulder holster under her coat. *Where are those assholes with the Mayor?*

***

Patch was in good physical shape. The much older Slay, not so much. Charging up the eight stories of stairwells was a challenge for the former homicide detective. Slay had to stop and catch his breath. "Go on. I'll be right behind you."

Patch gave him a look of concern, hoping he wasn't going to have to do CPR on his partner. "No problem. Catch up when you can." Patch started moving up the stairs at a near sprint, unencumbered by his slower partner.

Slay took a couple of minutes for his heart to slow down and to catch his breath. He cursed his diet, cigarette habit, age, and disdain for exercise as Patch disappeared up the blackness of the stairwell. "Fuck it." He took the mini flashlight out of his pocket and exited onto the fourth floor and looked for an elevator in the darkness.

CHAPTER 13

Bailey used the keys Mayor Henry provided to gain entrance to the side door. Behind him, Jones, Cara, Gumby, and camera guy followed. As soon as the door closed behind them, Gumby flicked on his flashlight and checked the room.

"That looks like blood on the wall... and there's a gun."

"What the hell?" Bailey examined the spatter. It appeared someone got their head cracked against the wall and there was a few more drops of blood on the floor nearby. And a Beretta 92 that might have been kicked off to the side.

"Somebody was here before us," Bailey said. "Jones, heads up. Keep Cara safe."

Camera guy whined. "What about me?"

For a moment, Bailey pondered what additional steps should be taken for camera guy's safety before making a recommendation. "Gumby, tell camera guy to shut the fuck up."

Gumby relayed the message. "Shut the fuck up, camera guy."

Camera guy looked sad, but he *did* shut the fuck up.

Jones snatched up the pistol and put it in his belt, then took point as the team advanced to the elevators.

***

The short, stocky man and his two thugs confronted the mayor as he stepped off the elevator onto the top floor of City Hall outside his office. "I'm afraid you need to come with us Mister Mayor."

The mayor could see there were three of them. The reflection of the red emergency lights made them glow like demons. But he wasn't afraid. This time he was ready.

From out of the shadows, the thin woman appeared behind them. "Yes, Mister Mayor. It's time to make amends with Mister Bangor."

The Mayor, with confidence bolstered by his new weapon, decided that he had been pushed around enough by Bangor and these two so-called 'handlers.' Defiantly, he said the scariest thing he could think of to say. "Do you feel like making my day, you, uh, punks?" Those words sounded better in his head. *Did I even say that right?*

He awkwardly reached for the weapon on his belt, but never having practiced, he struggled to get his hand on the grip. The stocky man slapped him solidly with an open hand across the back of the head, knocking him face down onto the floor, then he stomped on the Mayor's gun hand, grinding his foot on it hard enough to break fingers. The mayor squealed in pain.

The tall, thin woman laughed as she came over and yanked the gun from his nylon belt holster. "Nice try, loser." She addressed the men. "Take him to the roof."

They headed for the stairwell leading to the roof, when a startled Sergeant Patch opened the stairway door, not expecting to find four gun thugs and the mayor blocking his way.

Instinctively, the tall, thin woman fired with the Mayor's gun still in her hand, hitting Patch, causing him to fall backwards down the stairs. She led her men and the Mayor to the roof.

"Shit. That dead cop could ruin everything," the stocky man said.

The woman replied, "No it won't. We just say the mayor shot him. It's perfect."

They got the struggling Mayor to the roof and took him to the edge.

"Time for a leap of faith, Mister Mayor," the tall, thin woman said.

***

The Chief of Police parked his city car outside the City Hall building. He noticed the power was out. He grabbed a flashlight out of the glove compartment before going in. The Chief decided to use his access card to enter via the side door to avoid the security cameras. *No way I'm trusting that sleazebag Mayor.*

He walked across the parking lot to the side entrance. The door was not secured, in fact, it was left ajar. *Lazy bastards forgot to lock it after a smoke break.*

He proceeded to the elevators on his way to the top floor.

***

Bailey and his group were stepping off the elevator on the top floor when the group text message from Sergeant Patch came through: *999 trap at least 5.*

Bailey barked orders, "Officer needs emergency assistance. Shit! Gumby, find Patch. Jones, protect Cara and Camera Guy."

The team fell into motion like a tactical unit that had trained together for years. They quickly cleared the floor.

Gumby found Patch, "How bad, buddy?"

"That bitch missed my vest and caught me in the shoulder. I think it broke something. I can't move but I'm okay. Go on, go get 'em. They went to the roof."

Gumby yelled, "I got Patch in the stairwell. He's okay." He began helping Patch get to his feet and up to the top floor office area with Jones.

At that moment, a distraught Slay came onto the floor on the service elevator. "It's all my fault. I fell behind."

Patch said, "Don't worry about it now, those bastards are on the roof."

Bailey growled, "Slay. Cover the camera guy, Patch, and Cara. Jones, on me."

Gumby, Jones, and Bailey formed up at the stairwell. That's when they heard the burst of gunfire and a scream.

The Roof

The Mayor begged for his life. "You can't kill me. I know too much."

The tall, thin woman paused to process his logic. "You realize, that's not how any of this works, right?" She tossed the Mayor's gun a few feet away out of reach on the roof so it would be found later as evidence, proving he shot the nosy cop. *No sense letting it go over the side with the Mayor where some random bum might pick it up.*

The Mayor rephrased his plea. "I mean, I won't talk. You might need me later. I can run cover for you."

The begging was interrupted by a deep baritone from across the roof. "No one needs any of you!"

The tall, thin woman was in shock. *Father Brannigan? He can't be real!*

An old man adorned in black clothing with long white

hair, a black floppy hat, and a flowing black cape stood fifteen yards away from them at the fire escape ladder holding a revolver in each hand. "I am Father Brannigan. Repent or Die!" His cape fluttered in the wind like a superhero from the movies.

The tall, thin woman leaned back and put her boot to the Mayor's fat ass, launching him over the side of the building like a chubby rocket. Then she dove for the stairwell door.

The mayor screamed all the way down, "I choose repent!" But gravity beat him to redemption.

Gumby, Jones, and Bailey had formed up at the last set of stairs leading to the roof. That's when they heard the bloodcurdling scream.

On the top floor, Camera Guy hit the record button just in time to catch the Mayor dropping from the roof through the floor to ceiling windows by where they were hiding. Cara got on the phone and demanded a live feed with the station.

The man calling himself Brannigan, with his long white hair and cape spread flapping behind him, opened fire, emptying both guns into Bangor's hoodlums. The short, stocky man and one of the hired goons fell off the ledge with the Mayor, each taking fatal hits. Two others dropped straight down dead where they stood, mortally wounded, riddled with Brannigan's .44 special rounds. None of them had a chance to return effective fire. The mysterious priest stuffed his guns back in his belt and disappeared back down the fire escape. The confrontation began and ended in seconds.

Bailey, Gumby and Jones sprinted up the stairs as the tall, thin woman ran down. She wasn't expecting more cops. She ran head on into Bailey, knocking him back into Gumby. They fell backwards.

She pulled her Glock, but Jones sidestepped and reached over the top of the others, snatching the Glock out of her hand like a soaring eagle snatching a fish out of a river. Then, he whacked her across the face with the barrel of his machine gun like a nightstick, knocking her unconscious and sending some of her teeth tinkling against the wall.

Bailey noticed her shoes, black Chanel loafers. "That's our perp. She's one of the bum killers."

Gumby got to his feet and cuffed the woman behind her back and zip tied her feet. "I'd venture to guess she will be ordering the soup in prison." They moved up to the roof.

Two dead bodies. Shot to pieces.

They looked over the ledge.

Dead Mayor.

Dead hoods.

Gumby said glumly, "Someone is going to have to write a report on this."

Bailey said, "Don't worry, Gumby. It won't be us. Nobody is even going to know we were here." He called Ma Donna. "This is your anonymous tip calling, Ma. Send your people up. They need to discover this crime scene." He disconnected without waiting for a response.

Jones asked, "But who shot these turds?"

Bailey's face went blank. "Oh... yeah. Who *did* shoot these turds?"

Jones and Gumby shrugged.

Bailey said, "Well, the main thing is, *somebody* shot

these turds." He still wasn't comfortable with the possibility of a phantom shooter loose in the building.

Bailey noticed the junk pistol near the ledge that didn't seem to fit the scene. The dead hoods were pros. They had professional weapons. His cop instincts told Bailey he needed to pick up the cheap piece of hardware and stick it in his belt. He did.

The group went back down the stairwell to the top floor. On the stairwell they passed Cara and Camera Guy. Bailey said to them, "There's a great story up there, Cara. Ma Donna and her squad will be up here to make a statement in about five minutes. Have fun. Oh, and we have a live prisoner. Be sure not to step on her on the way up."

Cara gave Bailey a long kiss. "Thanks, Bailey. You really know how to show a girl a good time."

Outside the Mayor's office Slay was treating Patch's wound with the first aid kit from the supply room. He looked up at Bailey, "It might be a broken clavicle. It hurts but he'll be okay."

Patch asked. "What the hell happened up there?"

"I guess Gumby was right. The city fell."

"What?"

"Go up and take a look after the medics show up and get you stable. You probably won't see a crime scene like this again the rest of your career."

Bailey started to light a cigarette, in violation of many city policies he didn't care about right now, when the elevator dinged, and Police Chief Hinkley stepped off.

Utterly surprised, the Chief took a look around, realized the Mayor probably ratted them both out, and turned to get back on the elevator.

But the doors had snapped closed.

Cut off, he spun and ran for the stairs.

Bailey yelled, "I'll take him. The rest of you get out of here." pursued him.

Neither man was very fast, the Chief was an obese slob, and Bailey had a lot of miles on his odometer. But after two floors, the Chief was far enough ahead that Bailey was afraid the Chief might exit the poorly lit stairwell into the building somewhere and escape. He drew his weapon and yelled with what breath he could muster, "Freeze, Hinkley."

The out of shape, blubbery Chief Hinkley, winded and exhausted from the short chase, stopped at the top of a flight of stairs and turned with his hands up. "I'm the Chief of Police. You can't get away with pulling a gun on me."

"I'm a citizen review board commissioner. I can do all kinds of stuff."

"No, you can't." The Chief tried to read Bailey's face, to see his determination, but all he could see was the shape of a man barely illuminated by dull red glow from the emergency stairwell lights. The Chief decided he was facing a bluff he could call. He lowered his hands and reached for his own weapon. "I'm placing you under arrest for obstruction of justice and aggravated assault... *former* lieutenant Bailey."

Bailey thought, *maybe I did push this too far*.

Out of the red filtered darkness, from a place of concealment in a perch at the top of the stairwell landing structure, a figure dropped from above and landed behind

Bailey in a crouch. It was a man, also barely visible in the shadows of the eerie glimmer of the emergency lights. A caped figure slowly rose to his full height, appearing to be over nine feet tall with the big black floppy black hat and holding a revolver in each of his upraised hands. He was a silhouette of death, visible only to Hinkley.

"It is I, Father Brannigan! Repent or die, you fat thieving bastard!" the figure announced in the deepest baritone ever heard, issuing his demand from what sounded like the bowels of hell.

Bailey thought, *I know that stupid fake voice*, as he turned in disbelief.

The sudden appearance of the vengeful Vatican vigilante startled the hell out of Chief of Police who screamed like a little girl finding a lizard in her purse. The Chief took a step back, slipped, and lost his footing. He questioned, "You can't be real!"

Father Brannigan shouted back, "I am as real as Liberace, you heathen!"

Bailey withheld the urge to snicker. *This knucklehead hasn't changed one bit.*

The teetering chief appeared confused. That didn't sound priest-like.

The Brannigan figure lurched at the Chief like a well-armed tactical Dracula. "Sinner!"

The Chief squealed in fear as his feet flew completely out from under him. The corrupt law enforcement executive fell backwards awkwardly, swinging his arms like propellers without result. He tumbled haphazardly to the right, missed the step, then fell and landed eight feet down the stairwell on his neck with an excruciatingly loud crack. His eyes glazed over, and his tongue slid out to the corner of his mouth, dripping with drool.

The deep voice switched to a very normal voice and said, "Uh oh. It looks like you killed another chief, partner."

"Quintero."

"The one and only."

"What in the Sam Hell are *you* doing here?"

Quintero replied disinterestedly, "Oh, the usual. You know, wild card stuff."

"So, it was *you* at the church?"

"It was me everywhere, pendejo."

"Some things never change. But what the hell, man? Why didn't you just call?"

"Look, Frank. I'd like to reminisce, but I don't have a lot of time. I got a call from Hank... I mean Mayor Henry. He said you were going to cause some trouble and would need my help. So, I came out of retirement as a crime fighting superhero and went undercover, leveraging your Father Brannigan bullshit story. I've been working covertly ever since. Janitor, caterer, landscaper, bum, finally as Father Brannigan himself."

"That explains a lot. But I still got a whole lot of explaining to do. We have a real shit show here, and I'm not sure we have the evidence to back all this shit up if somebody doesn't spill. And it doesn't look to me like the Mayor and Chief are going to be talking to a prosecutor or the FBI anytime soon."

"Don't worry, Frank. I've been in City Hall every night as a janitor going through computers. It's all there. I found enough on the Mayor's computer to hang the chief too, so all your guys need to do is tell the truth. That asshole just slipped and fell while trying to escape."

"That's not the truth."

"It's pretty close."

"I'm not sure that's enough."

Quintero noticed the cheap gun stuffed in Bailey's belt and pointed to it. "Is that gun from the roof?"

"Yeah."

"It's the Mayor's. Give it to me."

Bailey handed him the weapon. Quintero planted it in the Chief's hand.

"Now, just say you were never here. And as far as the world knows, this dumbass just happened to slip and fall. It's not exactly the truth, but it saves you answering a lot of questions. It looks to me like he shot Patch, and then he helped that skinny woman throw the Mayor off the roof."

"She won't say that."

"It won't matter what she says. She's a dirtbag and you were never here. This lump just slipped and fell down the stairs because he's an uncoordinated slob and its dark. Everyone will *want* to believe that. He was the second most hated man in town after the Mayor."

"I *guess* that works. After Jones clocked her in the melon with that big old hairy machine gun, she probably won't be sure how she even got here tonight."

"Of course it works. Oh, I almost forgot. I have another bad guy in the sub-basement. He's tied up. He might need assistance and some clean shorts."

"Sub-basement?"

"Where the emergency generator wiring connects to the main power line. It's a real place. He's down there."

"I'll tell Ma to go get him." Bailey was still in shock at seeing his old partner so long a time. "It's been over twenty years, and you're just going to pop in, save the day, and what, disappear again? And you faked your death. What the hell was that about?"

"No, I really did die."

"Asshole."

Quintero laughed. "It's what I do. If you need a wild card again, I'll be there.

"I'll count on it."

"But please, never mention I was in town. I don't want to have to worry about some jerk with a *badge and no sense of humor* getting a hold of this story. There is no statute of limitations on... you know... stuff."

"Yeah, I know. I've been told that quite a few times lately." Bailey hugged his old partner. "Thanks, man."

Quintero peeled off his wig, hat, and cape to reveal a medic shirt and pants underneath. He bundled the guns and costume up into the cape and pulled a blue ball cap with a medic emblem out of a cargo pocket. "I'll be looking forward to the next time, brother."

Bailey smiled. "Right, but until then, Quintero," he looked down the stairway at the dead chief, "what do you recommend I do with..."

He looked around and Quintero was gone.

Shit.

***

Cara and Camera Guy were broadcasting the details of Ma Donna and her Detective Division Burglary Squad's corruption investigation, the death of the Mayor and the Chief, Father Brannigan's valiant effort to save the mayor, and the mysterious money man behind the real estate scam as well as the bum murder cases. It was worth an Emmy, if not a Pulitzer. The perfect end to Cara's journalism career and launch of her political career.

Bailey returned to the top floor, imagining an old medic walking nonchalantly out of the building and disappearing into the night. He passed the chaos and went to the mayor's conference room. Taking a deep breath, he gazed out the window over the city, as he did with Mayor Henry just a short time ago, remembering back to when the three of them wore badges and worked the streets, protecting the city, and bending every rule in the book. He remembered guys like Chuck, Larry, Pat, and Jim. He hung his head and silently said a rare prayer. *Thank you. Thank you for those times we had.*

Times gone by.

Then it was his turn to disappear from the scene.

Bailey's Apartment

The following night, the entire team celebrated surviving the case, the kind of party that has more drinking and enthusiasm than merely closing a case. No one in the police administration knew about the ad hoc team of investigators who *really* broke the case, successfully concealing around two hundred separate policy violations and acts of insubordination. All the credit went to an anonymous snitch and Ma's burglary squad, as well as Father Brannigan, also a hero in the case. Rumor had it that he had apparently returned to the Vatican, which in turn, denied his existence, as was expected when dealing with international secret agent priests.

Bailey said, "Ma, sorry your guys didn't get to wrap up

the case themselves."

"That's okay. The Bureau and the State AG took the whole thing over. But they kept my guys on as part of a task force, so they still got some status out of it. It's all cool. Oh, and everybody got a nice letter too."

"Did the Feds tell you what happened?"

Ma said, "The two worms in custody ratted out everything on everyone immediately."

"All those so-called tough guys fold like a deck chair when the real pressure's on." Slay commented. "It never fails."

Ma continued, "And their boss, that Bangor dude, is supposedly in a non-extradition country trying to make ends meet with a half-a-billion in Crypto he had squirreled away for a rainy day. Poor thing."

Cara said, "I'm not worried. He'll get his. We've heard the last of that guy."

Gumby gave Cara an almost unnoticeable cautionary glance but said nothing.

Bailey raised a glass. "Jones, Slay, Gumby... I'm sorry you guys didn't get credit for your work on this case, but I think it is best for all of us to stay off the radar and make this thing look as by-the-book as possible."

Patch, with his PD blue sling over his wound, said, "At least I get to be hero for accidently walking into a murder conspiracy and getting shot. Sorry I couldn't spread the glory around."

That earned him some lighthearted boos and jeers from the team.

Ma said, "You're going to milk that wound through the next six ex-wives it scores you, Patch. Admit it."

Ma got a laugh from everyone with that comment, because it was probably true. Patch just grinned and tipped a beer in a salute.

Slay said, "I'm just bummed we didn't get to meet Father Brannigan. The dude is legend."

Ma said solemnly, "Perhaps the greatest cop who ever lived."

Patch said, "I can't believe I almost saw him. Just a few seconds off and I might have been there when he shot it out with that gang. Can you just imagine?"

Bailey squirmed in his chair. Any mention of Father Brannigan made him uncomfortable. "The main thing is that no one knows it was us who broke this case. I don't know how command staff would take all the policy violations. And if the county prosecutor knew all the stuff we did, it might not be a happy ending. Not saying any of it was criminal."

Ma chirped, "And not saying it wasn't."

Jones stood up, held his beer up high, waited for silence, and dropped a truth bomb. "We didn't want any recognition, Lieutenant. We wanted to save the police department. And if that meant helping you kill another corrupt chief, then that's what we had to do." He paused and looked over the team. "To Blue Moses."

The team chanted back, "To Blue Moses," followed Jones' toast.

Bailey objected, "Yeah, but I didn't really *kill* the Chief, Jones."

"*Right.*"

Bailey became overly defensive. "I didn't. He just slipped and fell."

Slay weighed in. "Sure, whatever you say, Lieutenant."

"He *did* fall."

Patch said, "I mean it's not like there were any witnesses, so, whatever you say, sir."

"Patch, it was an accident. I'm serious."

Ma jumped on the bandwagon. "Of course you're serious. And it ain't like it's a regular murder. It's more of a third-degree manslaughter. If that was even a thing."

"That's *not* a thing," Bailey said, a bit louder than necessary.

"*Right.*"

"Dammit, I didn't kill the Chief."

"Nobody is saying you did, sir," Gumby clarified. "Not to your face. But that *is* two for two. Definitely a record of some sort."

Cara rescued him with a hug. "He's not a Chief Killer. Frank's just a teddy bear. You guys need to quit picking on him."

Jones asked, "So, what's next for us, Lieutenant?"

"Next, we lay low for six months. Things are cool right now. I'm still on the Citizen Review Board. We'll hopefully get a new police chief, this time from *within* the department. Maybe Deputy Chief Spooner, he seems like a real cop. Oh, and Father Garcia keeps his church right where it is. Everything is as it should be. So, we just chill out and wait for the heat to die down. But within six months, I feel like something new will come up that might require the immortals to reconvene."

Ma proposed a toast. "To the immortals."

The gang all happily clicked glasses to the new name.

Gumby said grimly, "I venture to predict, a different kind of crime wave will be upon us by then. Something new. Something bigger than this last one … And it might be the last case, for one of us."

Patch grouched at him. "Just wow, Gumby. You really know how to ruin a good party, man."

"I just meant someone might retire after it. All you guys are old. Not as old as the lieutenant, but pretty old."

Bailey spoke up, "Hey, I ain't *that* old."

Ma asked, "How old *are* you, lieutenant?"

Cara answered for him. "He's old enough to know better. But experienced enough to know how."

"How what?" Jones asked.

Cara winked. "I'll never tell."

EPILOGUE

The cold nights of the bum murder case long over. Summer was coming, and with it would come the kind of heat that can melt all the polish off of a cop's shoes after fifteen minutes of directing traffic. The office chatter about Father Brannigan, Possum Baby, and City Hall corruption had finally died down. Deputy Chief Spooner had been sworn in as the new Chief and there was peace at the PD for the first time in a long time.

Gumby and Jones were taking a coffee break on one of the last cool evenings left. Usually, the pair didn't say much. They just sipped coffee and stared into their cups.

Tonight, that changed.

"I know why Bailey had you find that big old hairy machine gun, Jones," Gumby said out of the blue.

Jones didn't immediately respond. He took a sip of coffee, snatched a toothpick out of the holder, peeled the paper off, and worked on an imaginary piece of food in his teeth before speaking. "I know to, Gumby. He said it was for lore. Police departments need folklore for their culture. The people got to believe that there are cops who will stop at nothing to protect the public. Bad guys need to believe it to. Even cops need to believe that somewhere on the department there's some lunatic cop willing to do anything and risk everything to get the job done. It's called hope. Bailey told me officers will tell my machine gun story around choir practice campfires for a hundred generations of cops. And it's true as shit. Although, if anyone asks, it never happened. That's how folklore works. Department moral hasn't never been this high since I started working here."

Gumby leaned in and lowered his voice to a whisper. "Yeah, that's all true, Jones. But there's more," he said secretively.

Now Jones was curious. "Like what?"

"The next case the immortals get."

"Yeah?"

Gumby pushed his glasses up on his nose with his index finger. "I venture to predict we are going to need it."

THE END

ABOUT THE AUTHOR

Daniel Byram

Daniel Byram is a retired police lieutenant with over 23 years of service in Mesa, Arizona, where he honed his expertise in investigations and leadership. Drawing from those frontline experiences, he has authored  more than 20 gripping mysteries and thrillers, including The Chief Killer, a tale of a veteran officer's final stand against corruption. Byram's stories blend high-stakes drama with themes of justice and resilience.

Beyond writing, he is an artist and business consultant. As a consultant, he advises on startups, training, and negotiations. Learn more at danielbyram.com.

PRAISE FOR AUTHOR

Daniel Byram is a present day Joseph Wambaugh, complete with the cynical worldview born from decades of dealing with crime, criminals and victims, but also possessing a remarkable sense of humor and irony to delight everyone! Hell, it makes old retired cops like me laugh and remember the camaraderie of police work and the heroes behind the badge, along with the remarkable adventures of true crime fighting.

If wound ballistics textbooks had plots, Dan Byram would have to be the author!

- DAVE "BUCK SAVAGE" SMITH IS AN INTERNATIONALLY RECOGNIZED LAW ENFORCEMENT SPEAKER, TRAINER, VIDEO PERSONALITY, AND AUTHOR.

This is Dan's best book yet. There's no other way to say it. "The Chief Killer" is real, I know, I was there. I spent many nights in the Florentine Room, walked a night beat in the downtown alleys, investigated the murders and worked with a 'Lt. Bailey' and a few other lieutenants like him. The Bailey's of policing are real, and the reason good cops get to do their jobs. Even though the events take place in Mesa, Arizona, if you're a cop you'll know the players, places, crimes, and politics. While big cities get the credit for doing "real" police work, it's the thousands of other cops all over America, like the characters in The Chief Killer, who are the ones out on the street every day kicking ass, taking names, throwing criminals in jail to make the streets safe while often fighting the system in order to survive and "To Protect and Serve." You know who they are. "The Chief Killer" is real, a fun read, worth your time, and for me it brought back a lot of memories. I miss the Florentine Room and working for Lt. Bailey.

- BILL RICHARDSON
RETIRED, MASTER POLICE OFFICER II
CRIMINAL INTELLIGENCE UNIT
MESA POLICE DEPARTMENT

BOOKS BY THIS AUTHOR

The Cold Blue Darkness

In 1989 Mesa PD, the Special Investigations Unit is besieged with street crime, internal local politics, and a mysterious figure committing bizarre acts within city buildings. But in the background, detectives cope with personal loss, impending retirement, and internal torment. Dark humor clashes with harsh reality as the bizarre becomes real and the real becomes bizarre.

Murder Me Last

MURDER ME LAST
Joey Catalina is a piece of filth, but he can pay half in advance.

Ex-cop turned private-eye Franky Fargo makes a living in the seedy underbelly of downtown San Diego. Life is tough, but it gets a little tougher when scumbag Joey Catalina walks into his office begging for help along with a bag of cash, a beautiful woman, a killer on his tail.
Eventually, every player in town comes to Fargo for

help... usually after it's too late.

The Magic Killers

When magician Nicolo DeCarlo's assistant goes missing, he calls his old friend Becker, a Fort Lauderdale private investigator. But finding the missing woman is one thing, having random hoods, thugs, and criminals trying to kill you is something else. Especially if you don't know why. A Becker Novel written by Daniel Byram under the pen name 'Bronco Hammer'